Nothing but a

Speck of Light

Left in the Dark

I0676311

by

A. Rose

ISBN: 979-8-9946135-0-4
Printed in the United States of America

Content Advisory

This work of fiction explores dark psychological themes, including violence, trauma, dissociation, mental health struggles, and thoughts of self harm. Some scenes may be unsettling or intense. Reader discretion is advised.

Explicit content: recommended for 18+ readers

Please read with care.

For my family, who always believed in me.

For Adrian, the best little brother anyone could ask for.

And for Chad, who inspired me to start writing my first book.

If you ever find yourself lost in a room without a single spark—look closer.

The light wasn't ever missing. It was you.

one

I was never proud of my name. I didn't like it printed anywhere. That's Clay's rule, not mine.

"Mystique sells better," he once whispered.

Or maybe I imagined it.

The world reads *C. Holloway* and wonders who I am. Hell, I wonder too.

Under my real name, Nick Smith, I publish safe stuff. Literary. Predictable.

Boring.

But these stories… the ones that creep into my head and bleed onto the page?

They belong to someone else.

I can never remember drafting the books. They just exist, perfectly written, exactly where they're supposed to be. Not mine. But mine.

The manuscripts already uploaded, encrypted, routed through enough proxies to make them untraceable.

Third time.

Third time this happened.

Third time I've stared at a story that could've only come from someone else, someone who knows too much. Someone who knows me.

Not Alone by C. Holloway.

She thought she was alone. That was her mistake.

My stomach twisted. My hands shook. I skipped ahead.

No one will find her. But the bugs already have.

I didn't write that. I couldn't have. And yet... my chest tightened as if I'm holding my breath for the first time in years. The first time since her.

The first book... connected to her. My ex. Her murder. The memory clawed at me, sharp and unrelenting.

Just another story about a lifeless victim by the lake. Not real. Not me. That's what I tell myself. But the unease curled firm in my ribs, whispering I can't pretend anymore.

My pizza's cold. The clock on my desktop glowed 3:44 a.m. I must've fallen asleep at my desk again. The house was quiet, except for the hum of the fridge and the soft clink of ice melting in a glass I didn't remember pouring.

I switched tabs, leaving behind the girl who was never alone. Back to the safe stuff.

I saved and sent my manuscript to my publisher. *Free the Robots* by Nick Smith. A dystopian tale about sentient machines rising... because apparently that's what sells now.

My hands lingered over the keyboard, trembling slightly. I should be relieved. I am relieved. And yet, there's an icy tangle of fear fixed around my ribcage.

I took a stretch in my computer chair, staring at the ceiling wondering how my book got completed.

Vibrations started buzzing as my phone went off at the end of the table. My thoughts disintegrated into the back of my mind.

It was Betty from the publishing house.

"You finally finished it!" she said. "I was starting to worry."

Me too.

"I know you've been struggling to finish the book, so it must feel great that it's done."

"Ya..."

She cut me off. "Well, go ahead and get some

rest, you deserve it. I'll manage getting every-thing ready on my end."

I *should* get rest. My book was finished, and that's all that mattered.

I got up and crawled into bed trying to ignore the girl who was never alone.

My eyes closed as I struggled to fall asleep. I tried counting backward from one hundred because my therapist told me it would help. It didn't.

The third book.

Another nightmare.

I can't shake it.

***

It's been a week since the books were published, and now, I'm sitting with my therapist in a lightly dimmed room pretending to listen.

There's a strange painting on the wall—one of those abstract pieces that's supposed to make you think and reflect. It just made my stomach turn. I focused on the other one instead: a single speck of light followed by darkness. Fitting.

I didn't feel hopeful today.

Dr. Ames adjusted her glasses. "You've been quiet since your last session. How are you feeling... after the release?"

"It's just a book," I said.

"You've published before, but this one seemed harder to finish."

I shrugged. "Guess I was overthinking it."

She watches me. She's always watching me, like she knows I'm leaving things out. Which I am.

She knows I write, but she doesn't know who I write as. She doesn't know that "C. Holloway" is the name on some of the books I publish, or that I don't remember writing half the words that make me successful.

She doesn't know about the blackouts.

"I've been sleeping more," I say, which is technically true. I just didn't mention that I've also been waking up to open Word documents I don't remember creating.

Dr. Ames tapped her pen against her knee.

"Have you been experiencing any... dissociation lately? Gaps in memory, lost time?"

Too close.

I forced a laugh, "What, like I'm sleepwalking around town?"

She didn't smile, "I'm serious, Nick."

I avoided her eyes, "I've been tired, not... crazy."

The ticking clock in the background was louder than normal.

"Crazy isn't a word I'd use," she says. "But exhaustion can cause dissociation. So can trauma. Even creative overload."

My hands are clammy. I wiped them on my jeans.

"If anything comes up," she added gently, "you can talk to me. You don't have to keep it all in your head."

I nodded. But I don't say a word.

Because if I say it aloud, it becomes real.

"Same time in two weeks then?" she says.

The clock on the wall struck four.

Already?

"See you then."

I left her office with more questions than answers. I told her I'm only tired. That I haven't been sleeping well. She believed me. Or maybe she didn't.

***

I didn't go home right after therapy. Instead, I met up with Adam—detective, skeptic, my closest thing to a brother.

We met at the usual spot, a diner on 12th that still had those sticky menus and bottomless coffee. The place smelled like overused grease and burnt toast. He already had a plate of fries in front of him.

"You look like shit," he said as I slid into the seat across from him.

"Appreciate the warm welcome."

He smirked, "So... still stuck on your dystopian novel or whatever it is you're writing now?"

I stirred the coffee the server had just dropped off.

"I finished something recently."

Adam's eyebrows lifted. "Seriously? I thought you were in a slump."

"I was," I said. "It came to me all at once."

"Lucky you."

He popped a fry into his mouth. "What's it about?"

"Just... dystopian fiction about freedom for technology."

"Gee, thanks for the thrilling synopsis."

I didn't respond. I don't like lying to him, but the truth was worse.

Adam leaned back, forks idle on his plate. "Had a weird case the other day. Rookie came in rambling about another C. Holloway drop online. The girl in the book? Dead ringer for that podcaster who went missing months ago. Too damn close."

I froze, willing my face into stone. Fragments of the book flickered in my mind, snippets I couldn't shake.

"Creepy stuff," Adam pressed. "Reddit's already on fire. People think the guy's a retired cop... or just a lunatic with too much time."

I cleared my throat. "Could be coincidence."

Adam leaned forward, eyes narrowing. "You believe that? Did you read his books? The details line up in ways you don't ignore. If this keeps happening..."

I sipped my coffee, forcing calmness while a tightening clawed at my core. "I skimmed a little. It's hard to read."

Adam chewed, never looking away. "Still hits close to home, though, doesn't it?"

I forced a smile, brittle as glass, "Sure. But they're just stories. At least, that's what I tell myself."

A memory claws at the edges of my mind, a woman screaming, the smell of iron. My throat stiffened.

Adam's gaze pinned me. "Cop, psycho, or someone who knows too damn much and I don't like it."

I set my mug down before Adam notices my hands shaking. "I try not to think about it."

His jaw flexed, "Nick, that first book wasn't fiction. I don't care what anyone says. The way it matches what happened, it's like he's mocking us. Mocking you."

The lump in my throat was stone. "Maybe," I muttered, wishing the conversation would end.

Adam leaned closer, voice a growl. "I don't trust anyone who writes shit like this. You understand?"

My chest thundered. I nodded, eyes on the black swirl of coffee in front of me.

***

After meeting with Adam, all I want is to get home. The sky bruises with late afternoon clouds as I drive. My mind feels fogged, like a heavy blanket smothering every thought. Memories I don't want to resurface claw at the edges of my consciousness.

Once inside my house, the faint smell of old books and brewing coffee greets me, but it does little to calm the storm inside. I stumble to the bathroom and splash freezing water on my face, the sharp chill trying to cut through the haze.

How is this possible?

I sit at my desk and open my laptop, the soft hum of the fan filling the quiet room. Since Adam mentioned the missing podcaster earlier—the one whose description eerily matches the character in *Not*

Alone—I can't shake the uneasy feeling building in my stomach.

The screen's pale glow flickers across my face as I pull up the digital copy. My eyes race over the words, desperate to find the passage that unsettles me so deeply.

And then it's there:

She has long brown hair that catches the sunlight in a soft glow, hazel eyes full of quiet kindness. Freckles scatter across her cheeks like the sun has kissed her.

My breath hitched in my lungs.

I pull my laptop closer, the light washing over the dim room. Fingers resting lightly on the keyboard, I open a tab and search: local news, missing persons.

Her photo appears, too crisp, too carefully lit, like it has been pulled straight from a press kit. A practiced smile frozen mid-expression. I'm not ready to see her there. Part of me had hoped she wouldn't still be listed as missing. Clara Whitman.

She'd interviewed me once, almost two years ago. A long-form podcast—quiet studio, dim lights, her voice warm and patient as she guided the conversation where she wanted it to go.

We'd talked about writing. About grief. About Claire. It was the first time—and the last time—I publicly voiced my thoughts on her murder. I can recall thinking how smoothly the conversation had flowed.

She was good at her job, more than good. She had a way of listening that made you feel heard, asking questions that made you think but never cornered you. I left the studio that day feeling lighter than I had in years, like someone had finally made the space safe enough for me to speak, to open up.

I remember thinking people like that—wasn't something you came across often. I didn't dwell on it then, I just knew I felt better walking out than I had walking in.

After the episode aired, she kept in touch. Occasional emails. A message here and there, checking in, floating the idea of a follow-up. I agreed, eventually. Told myself it was professional. Harmless.

Now she was missing.

Last seen leaving the studio late one night. No signs of a struggle. No obvious reason for her to vanish at all.

What gripped at my stomach wasn't just her missing; it was the reminder that people around me kept disappearing. Now her.

They were different relationships, but the same echoing loss. And she hadn't deserved any of it. None of them had.

My vision wavers. The room pitches sideways. A tense fist wraps around my throat, squeezing until I gag, my lungs dragging in air that feels thick as mud.

Flashbacks surge, crashing like waves I never knew were real. Memories I thought were only my imagination—now vivid, raw.

I snap the page closed and slam the laptop shut, the sudden darkness pressing in. Outside, the wind whispers against the windowpane. The silence thickens, almost suffocating.

I tell myself it's nothing. Just my mind playing tricks.

But deep in my gut, a cold certainty settles like frost. Someone is watching.

Waiting.

And whatever comes next, I'm not sure I'm ready to face it.

***

Sweat soaks through my clothes and onto the sheets. I'm having a nightmare about her again. A loud thud on the window snaps me awake. Rapid thumps pound in my chest, mimicking the drums of a dark orchestra.

For a second, I can't place where I am. The softness of dawn peeks through the curtains, but the smell of the lake, dust, and old wood hits me all at once.

Another sound. Softer this time. A scrape against the window.

I force myself up, legs stiff, my head pounding. I walk through my tilted living room toward the window. I lean against the wall, gently pull the curtains back, and see it: a bird, small and black, lifeless on the front porch.

One wing twists at an unusual angle; the neck bends like a snapped twig. The faintest flutter of its broken wing twitches once more, like a final plea.

My eyes lock on its stillness, like it never saw the end coming. My throat fixes the same way it did when I was twelve, hiding around the corner.

I swallow hard, the old panic rising from the pit of my core—the kind that used to grip me when I heard the screams. A memory I don't want to revisit. I blink hard and look away, but the image clings, like it's burned into the back of my eyelids.

While I redirect my thoughts, I begin to wonder how I got here. I pour fresh orange juice and notice my fingernails. Dirt is packed underneath them. My hands tremble. I glanced down at my shirt. Something's smeared on the hem. Blood? It's dried. Old. But not mine.

A subtle breeze carries the scent of the lake water and something else—metallic. A smell that echoes through my memories.

In the distance, a faint noise grows louder and louder.

Then my alarm clock shatters the silence.

***

I woke up, drenched in sweat, again. I dreamt about the first time I started to really worry about losing my memories. Sometimes the lines blur. Dreams bleeding into reality, and reality slipping away like sand through my fingers.

It's been almost six years since it began. The memories truly started fading after Claire passed, my world shattered into fragments. At some point, I even bought a lake house… though I don't remember why or when.

I haven't told anyone.

Not even Adam. Not even Dr. Ames.

And something inside me is starting to remember.

It's now August, my least favorite month. Maybe it's the heat that's making me this irritable. It's been five months since I released anything under the name C. Holloway. The last book was *Not Alone.*

And Clara? She's still missing, out there somewhere.

No one's figured out who C. Holloway is.

Not yet.

I haven't written anything since. Haven't dared.

But some mornings, I wake up in front of the screen and there it is.

A new story, half formed. Typed out like someone else is pulling the strings.

***

I'm starting to get paranoid.

No, scratch that. I am paranoid.

I drive to the store with a hoodie and a hat pulled low over my face with sunglasses on like I was trying to dodge paparazzi, except no one's watching me.

I bought four security cameras. The guy at checkout made a joke about catching raccoons. I forced a small fake laugh; I wasn't very amused because I used to have a raccoon problem in my garage.

Back home, I started to install the cameras myself. Living room, hallway, outside the front door, and one aimed directly at my writing desk—my war zone.

Every time I drilled into the wall, I jumped. I felt eyes. Not from outside. Inside.

"There's no way I'm writing these," I muttered aloud, as if saying it would make it true.

Am I?

Maybe the footage would show me the truth.

Maybe it would catch the phantom typist or whoever was hijacking my life and spilling blood onto blank pages.

I was crouched under the desk, zip-tying a wire into place when I heard it.

A voice.

Low. Smooth. Disappointed.

Really, Nick?

The room's temperature seemed to drop, cold fingers tracing my spine.

My hand froze.

The breath I'd been holding escaped in a shaky gasp, but when I peeked around the room, nothing moved. The windows were shut. The house was still. Even the air felt thicker, heavier. Like the house was holding its breath with me.

It's in your head, I told myself.

It didn't help.

Then everything went dark. Like someone flipped a switch in my brain.

Next thing I knew, it was morning.

I woke up in bed.

Not passed out on the floor. Not crumpled in a chair.

In bed, under the covers.

Someone had tucked me in.

A chill ran through me as I realized I was clutching a rosary in my hand. The beads were warm, like I'd been holding them for hours. It wasn't the first time this had happened.

Sometimes I'd wake up with it tangled around my fingers, like someone or something was reminding me to pray.

Unease slowly pressed in as I sat up, the metal cross pressing into my palm. I stumbled toward my desk. The laptop was open. Still warm.

My inbox was open too.

There it was, uploaded to be traceless once again.

A new manuscript.

Quiet Now by C. Holloway.

I scrolled through it, heart pounding in my throat.

A. Rose

She was hard to keep quiet, but I made sure no one could hear her screams.

I felt the blood drain from my face as my hands went cold.

It was disturbing. Graphic. Dark.

Not my genre. Not my style.

And yet… the cadence, the flow, the fingerprints were somehow mine.

I quickly picked up my phone and scanned the footage taken from the cameras. The video showed me: Sitting calmly at the desk. Typing like I was possessed but at peace. Like I wanted to be there.

Not frantic. Not afraid.

Focused.

I watched myself leaning back in the chair, cracking my knuckles, and smiling. The corners of my mouth curled upward, too deliberate, rehearsed, like someone else was wearing my skin. There was a chill in that smile, a promise I didn't understand but felt deep in my bones. My breath hitched as the screen showed me doing things I couldn't remember wanting to do.

Smile.

The smile didn't feel like mine. I couldn't breathe. I backed away from the desk, hitting the bookshelf with a thud. My knees nearly gave out. How could I not remember any of this?

How could that be me?

I approached the keyboard again, hesitantly. Every instinct in me screamed to remove it. Burn it. Smash the laptop. Anything. But my hands wouldn't move.

Then a whisper. Clearer this time. Closer.

It felt like someone was right behind me.

You're finally doing something worth reading.

The words slithered into my ear, like it was poison.

My skin prickled, hairs rising as if warning me to run, but my feet felt glued to the floor.

I spun around.

Nothing.

Just my own empty hallway.

But the air felt heavy. Charged. Like static before a storm.

My skin crawled. I know I didn't write it. But deep down... a sliver of me wonders if I did.

I stared at the screen, numb, as the hours ticked by. Overnight, the manuscript started gaining traction.

Downloads, comments, shares. The numbers climbed faster than any of C. Holloway's earlier releases.

For a brief moment, a strange surge of pride bubbled up inside me. Someone out there was reading this. *Me,* in a way.

But the feeling was fleeting, swallowed quickly by a creeping dread. What if this was no longer about writing? What if it was something else entirely and I have no control over it.

I pulled out a fresh journal and started writing down everything that's been happening. Maybe if I put it all on paper, I can see the gaps more clearly, maybe even fill them in.

My pen stills.

Do I really want to go down this road? Investigate myself? There's no one I can talk to about it. No one knows what's going on except me… and even I'm not sure.

I closed the journal. If I write it down, it becomes real. And if it's real, then I'm crazy.

This isn't real. It can't be.

Instead, I'll just keep an eye on things, watch through the security feeds I installed. That's safer. This is all just in my head.

Deep down, I didn't want to be alone, but the walls of my house felt like they were closing in. I needed to escape—from my laptop, from my thoughts, from the heaviness at home.

***

Later that night, I stepped out into the cool air and made my way to a local bar. The dim glow of neon signs buzzed softly outside, and the low murmur of voices seeped through the door as I entered. I needed a drink.

As soon as I walked in, I spotted Adam nursing a beer at the far end of the bar. He was the last person I wanted to see, yet somehow, maybe he was exactly what I needed.

We've been best friends since high school and seeing him has always been comforting. But lately, talking to him has been hard. I hate lying to him, and hiding everything felt worse.

I took a deep breath, then approached the bar. "Is this seat taken?" I asked, sliding onto the stool next to him.

Adam looked up, surprise flickering in his eyes.

"Well, what the hell are you doing here? You rarely come out. Special occasion?" His grin was easy, familiar, and before I could answer, he flagged down the bartender. "Get him a drink. Put it on my tab."

I gave a small smile, grateful for the gesture. "I just needed to clear my head," I admitted, the truth spilling out more honestly than I intended.

The bartender returned with a glass of whiskey and coke, condensation beading on the cold glass. I took a sip, the sharp burn grounding me. "Thanks. I needed that."

Keep it together.

The thought was quiet, firm. I blinked and focused on Adam.

Adam laughed, "Anytime. Plus, you've got the next round." He leaned in a little. "So… what's going on? Trouble with the writing again?"

I hesitated, the words heavy on my tongue but needing to be said. "Writing's been making me feel crazy."

Adam leaned back, watching me too closely.

"Speaking of writing, that C. Holloway guy dropped another book last night. Got the alert this morning." His voice was casual, but his eyes weren't.

Answer him. Don't zone out.

Another thought slipped in, almost too casual to notice.

A grip squeezed in my chest. My pulse stuttered.

"Yeah?" I forced the word out, my throat dry.

"Yeah." He tilted his head. "Nick... I don't get how anyone reads that shit for fun. It's twisted. And it's getting worse."

I looked away, my gaze fixed on the condensation sliding down my glass. "People like what they like."

"That doesn't make it normal," Adam pressed, quieter now. "Sometimes I think the guy behind those books is... dangerous. Like he's not just making it up."

My fingers twitched against the tabletop. I wanted to laugh it off, deflect, but nothing came.

Adam sighed, softening. "I'm not trying to drag you into it. I just... I worry. You don't sleep. You've been isolating yourself. And then you got this crap author on top of it. It's not good for you, Nick."

"I know, but it's still considered fiction," I muttered. My hands balled into fists in my lap. "He is twisted, though."

Adam studied me, then let it go, easing back with a forced grin. "Alright, all right. No lecture. But hey, maybe try writing something new if your dystopian books get too boring. Hell, write a book about me. Bestseller guaranteed."

That broke through my guard. A real laugh escaped me. "An autobiography about you?"

"Damn right." He grinned, "Hero cop. Tragic backstory. Handsome as hell."

For a fleeting moment, it felt normal again. Safe. But the weight pressing in my chest never really loosened.

two

Sleep blurred the edges of the city house, but something already felt off. The place that felt like mine, cluttered with books, scattered notes, and the dull buzz of morning traffic outside. It was home.

The lake house was different. Far away, quiet, and still. A place I only visited when the weight of the world pressed too hard.

For now, though, I needed to focus on today. There were errands to run, coffee to drink, and a world that was, for the moment, normal.

It had been a month since C. Holloway's latest book, *Quiet Now,* went live. The numbers kept climbing, the kind of success that felt unreal given everything else. I'd been sleeping better than before, trying to savor the calm without overthinking it.

No more waking up to mysterious Word documents. No more coming to and finding myself half-lost at my desk, with the cursor blinking like it's taunting me.

I've been able to focus again, pouring myself into my dystopian fictions, letting the words flow without that shadow breathing down my neck. It's like I'd finally regained control. I feel… present. It's only been a month but maybe that last book was C. Holloway's final goodbye.

Quiet Now.

***

Lost in thought, I found myself wandering into Lucy's bookstore on the corner of 12th and Broadway, a place I'd been coming to for years. The smell of old paper and dust was oddly comforting; the shelves lined with the kind of hidden gems you never find online. I've known Lucy since we were kids.

Lucy was behind the counter, her chin resting on her hand. She perked up when she saw me, though there was a flicker in her eyes I couldn't quite read.

"Well, if it isn't Author Nick Smith," she said with a teasing smile, but there was an edge underneath it.

"Hey, Lucy," I said, trying to keep it casual. "Is everything okay?"

She hesitated, fiddling with the pen in her hand. "I just… I thought we were supposed to grab coffee a couple of weeks ago. You never showed up. I figured maybe something came up, but then you went quiet."

I blinked. "Wait, we had plans?"

Her smile faltered just a little, more hurt than angry. "Yeah. But it's fine. I know you get wrapped up in your work. I'm used to it."

Her words landed heavier than they should have. She's a childhood friend, so I don't just bail on her without explaining. But… I didn't remember making plans. A cold knot tightened my gut. What if I made plans and I'm forgetting, again?

My throat froze. I hated letting her down, hated the way my memory seemed to betray me.

"I'm sorry, Lucy. I'll make it up to you. But I'm going to meet with Adam right now, we'll talk later." I held her gaze, hoping she could see the sincerity in my eyes.

The bell above the door chimed faintly as I stepped back outside, the weight of her disappointment clinging to me as I headed toward the diner to meet Adam. He'd never cared much about books; as a detective, he never had the patience for them, so the shop might as well have been invisible every time he passed by.

***

The diner smelled like stale coffee and fried bacon, the kind of place with vinyl booths and the low hum of conversation that felt like comfort. Adam wasn't here yet, so I slid into our usual corner booth. The TV mounted near the ceiling is tuned to the evening news.

Suddenly, the background noise of clinking dishes and murmuring customers faded, replaced by the sharp, clipped voice of the newscaster reporting another murder.

Steady. You're fine. Focus.

The voice presses in, unnervingly calm, patient. I swallow hard, blink, and shake my head. No… it's just me, I tell myself. But the knot in my stomach doesn't loosen.

I whisper under my breath, "Please… no…" This wasn't new. I should've known it would happen again. But how? How could it?

A friendly pat on my shoulder from behind, jolted me back to the present.

"Hey man, sorry I'm late," Adam says, sliding into the seat across from me.

I didn't say anything right away. My eyes are fixed on the screen. He followed my gaze and nodded toward the news.

"That would be why," he muttered, his voice low.

I finally met his eyes. "Long day?" I asked, trying to keep my voice casual, to keep the dread from creeping in.

Adam ran a hand through his hair, glancing at the server as she approached. "A body was found," he says, nodding at her to bring his usual coffee. "And this time, we have a lead."

A lead? Already?

Strain builds in my ribs, as the old anxiety clawed its way back. I forced a calm tone. "Is it that messed-up author?"

Adam shook his head, a grim set to his jaw.

"Surprisingly, no. This one's different. Had one of my guys look over that new book C. Holloway released. The details don't match this case. It was someone else."

Relief crashed through me in waves. Maybe this was just a normal case. Maybe the chaos wasn't following me around anymore.

I told you, you're fine. Trust me more.

The words were calm, insistent, almost foreign in their certainty. I blinked, startled. Then I shook my head. No… it's just me trying to settle down. But the tension coiling in my chest loosened a little.

"That's great," I say, a little too quickly. Adam's eyes narrowed, studying me like he knew I was trying to convince myself.

I hastened to add, "I mean, that might mean this creepy author isn't murdering people?" My attempt at humor fell flat.

Adam paused, chewing thoughtfully. "Yeah, that's the last thing I need. Speaking of, have you read anything yet?"

I shrugged, "No, I haven't read much, just bits and pieces, but I saw his numbers climbing fast. I wonder who he is. Maybe I'll try reading one sometime." I tried to sound casual, as if it's not me who uploaded it.

Adam grimaced, "My colleague read me a scene last week. I'm a detective, but even I couldn't stomach it. Don't get why people dig this demented stuff."

I chuckled lightly, trying to deflect.

Adam leaned back, his fork clinking against his plate. "So, how's life been treating you lately?"

I hesitated before answering, and my thoughts tugged toward Lucy. "I ran into Lucy today. She said I bailed on coffee a couple of weeks ago." The memory builds pressure in my core.

Adam smirked, "Lucy again? The girl who disappears every time I show up?"

I laughed under my breath. "She doesn't disappear. She's just… not much of a people person. You know that."

"Nick, I've met her—what—four, maybe six times? Usually, she just mumbles a hello and slips out before I can even finish a sentence. The other times…" he shrugged, "well, it was just kind of awkward. Like when I went into her bookstore once to buy a gift for my wife. She was polite, helpful even, but definitely on the shy side, you know, for running a bookstore."

"She is shy," I say, quieter now. "That's just how she is and she manages."

Adam studies me for a moment, then leans back. "Alright, man. I just don't get how you two are so close. We've got plenty in common, and you'd think I'd get along with her too."

My fingers traced the worn scratches on the table. "We grew up together. That's different. It's not the same kind of bond you and I have."

Adam tilted his head, "A bond? Or do you just like her?"

"No. You know this." My voice thinned, "Remember in high school? You showed up right after I turned her down. That was awkward as hell, but… she got over it. We stayed friends."

Adam grinned, easing the weight in the air.

"Well, we're older now. And you haven't really dated anyone since—" He cut himself off, regret flickered across his face. "Sorry. Didn't mean to bring that up."

Tension pulsed through me. "It's fine. That was years ago. I'm moving forward." I find myself repeating a phrase he's heard too many times as I tossed him a smile that doesn't quite reach.

"Anyway," Adam says, shifting back to safer ground, "just apologize to Lucy. She'll get over it and come back around. Make it up to her."

"Thanks." Finally, a thought that didn't feel so heavy. "I'll do that."

I leaned back, exhaling slowly. Maybe he's right. It is that simple.

I had another fun time with Adam. It's rare to find someone I can just be myself around, someone who doesn't ask too many questions or expect too much. Talking with him made the weight of my worries lift, even if just for a little while.

***

As I stepped out of the diner, the late afternoon sun warmed my face. Across the street, the familiar sign of the bookstore caught my eye. Adam's words echoed in my head, and before I could second-guess it, I found myself crossing over.

The shop was quiet, filled with the soft scent of old paper and ink, as the sun streamed through the windows, and dust motes danced lazily in the air. I noticed Lucy wasn't behind the counter or anywhere in sight.

I started browsing the shelves, scanning through titles and authors, trying to find something that might catch my interest.

My feet led me toward a small table featuring popular books and bestsellers. And there it was: all four novels by C. Holloway, arranged side by side, from the very first release to the latest.

I must have stared at the books longer than I realized, my thoughts knotted and heavy. My mind fogged by the irony of it all when Lucy's voice broke through the silence.

"Nick, you okay?" she asked softly. Her tone was gentle, but her eyes carried something unreadable.

I turned and found her standing behind the counter, a small, almost shy smile tugging at her lips. I hadn't even heard her come out of the back room.

"You were spacing out again," she added, tilting her head.

Her gaze flicked to the table beside me.

"I was just browsing through the books," I said quickly, forcing a smile as I followed her glance.

Her eyes lingered on one of the covers, her fingers brushing against its edge like she couldn't help herself. "You know," she said slowly, "aside from that first one he released, his books aren't that bad."

I raised a brow. "You actually like this stuff?"

She nodded, searching for the right words.

"It's different. The way he writes—it's like stepping into someplace you're not supposed to be, but it feels… familiar. Scary, but thrilling. The details grab you and don't let go."

Her face lit up as she talked, and for a moment I just watched her, almost forgetting the nausea twirling in my stomach. There was a strange flicker of pride too, someone was a fan of my writing, even if I couldn't remember it.

No one really knows who C. Holloway is.

Lucy's voice dropped, her smile fading. "No one knows who C. Holloway is. No photos, no history. Just… nothing. Like he's some kind of ghost."

I gave a careless shrug, though my pulse quickened. "That's what I've heard."

Her hand hovered over *August Rush,* her thumb grazing the title before she drew in a breath. "Still, the details in this one… they're too close to—" She glanced at me, concern shadowing her expression.

"I know," I cut in, the words automatic, my throat tightening. "But it's just fiction."

She shook her head, eyes narrowing slightly.

"But who would write something like that? We've talked about it before, but it makes you wonder what the other books might be based on. I know Adam's been asking the same questions."

The air thickened between us. I looked at her, my expression hardening, silently begging her to drop it. Talking about this, an old wound always reopened and worse—it meant staring at the part of myself I could never remember. I didn't want to have this conversation. Not with her. Not with anyone.

She caught the look in my eyes and softened.

"I'm sorry. I know you hate talking about it. It's just… his books are getting so popular. And if we could figure out who he is, maybe—just maybe—it could help solve her case."

"I know." My voice came out thinner than I meant. "Everyone keeps saying that. But I just want to let go. Move on."

Lucy studied me for a long moment, her expression a mix of sympathy and something I couldn't quite name. "I get it. I can't imagine what you're carrying. You don't have to go through this alone."

"Thanks, Lucy." I forced sincerity into my words, though something churned in my gut.

"You've always been there. But I promise, I'll be fine."

Lucy leaned back, arms crossed, eyes distant for a moment. "It's been six years now, hasn't it? Time just slipping by."

I nodded, running a hand over my face. "Too long. I keep thinking about everything that happened, but I can't move forward. Not really." That was the first honest thing I'd said in a long time.

She tilted her head, her voice softening.

"Maybe that's the point. You're stuck because you never had closure. Because what happened back then was never fully faced. And until you let yourself see all of it—really face it. You're going to keep circling the same ground."

I swallowed, tension knotting in my chest.

"Closure… you mean, investigate?"

"I mean stop avoiding it," she said gently, leaning forward. Her eyes sharpened—not accusatory, just intent. "You've spent years pushing it to the back of your mind. The only way to move on is to look at it instead of running. To sit with it. To understand what you've been circling around all this time."

I let out a long breath. "This C. Holloway guy wouldn't bother me so much if his books didn't feel so… familiar. Like he's treading on something he shouldn't be."

Lucy shrugged, a small, uneasy smile tugging at her lips. "Then at least you'll know the truth. You won't be stuck wondering anymore. That kind of uncertainty… it eats people alive."

She hesitated, "I just worry about you, Nick."

I gave her a smile, brittle at the edges.

"You always have, since we were kids. I know I've been distant lately, but we'll hang out soon. Maybe we can—"

Don't deflect.

The thought slipped in quietly, almost reasonable.

She's been a good friend. You keep pulling away.

Don't do that again.

The words stalled. I stared at the floor, then shook my head.

My smile stayed fixed, but the unease curls in my chest. The thought hadn't felt like mine, yet it echoed as if it had always been there. A voice I hear often… but lately, I wonder if it's even mine.

Keep her close.

Lucy didn't speak right away. She watched me with quiet concern, the way she used to when we were younger.

"Hey," she said softly. "Are you okay?"

I forced a breath.

"Yeah. I just—I should get going."

Her lips pressed together.

"Just… don't fall back into old habits, Nick."

I paused.

"Old habits?"

She offered a small, careful smile, "Pulling away. Disappearing when things get hard."

I nodded, even though my pulse picked up.

"I won't."

She didn't look convinced.

"Just text me and we'll plan something. Promise I won't bail." I forced the words into a smile as I left.

***

When I got home, I dropped my bag onto the floor. The hollow thud echoed through the quiet room, making the silence press against my ears.

My head spun from the day. I should've remembered planning to meet Lucy, but that thought only made the gnawing in my core worse. Friends like her and Adam were rare. Lucky, even.

But another part of me—insistent, unbidden—whispered that none of this made sense. That part didn't feel like me.

My gaze drifted to my laptop. The air around it felt heavier, like it had been waiting. Should I open it? I already knew what was inside or at least, I thought I did. Still, some part of me, drawn by a force I didn't recognize, pushed forward.

I picked it up, flipping it open. My fingers hovered over the keys, trembling just enough that I almost pulled back. Against my better judgment, I typed in *August Rush.* The screen glowed to life, washing the room in a cold, blue haze.

Minutes bled into hours. I wasn't sure when the light outside faded, or when the first tremor of rain started tapping against the window. The clock on the nightstand blinked at 9:37, then 11:04, then 1:12. Somewhere between those numbers, I stopped keeping track.

I skimmed over the parts I knew, the ones I wrote. The rhythm of my sentences, the familiar ache of my own voice. But when the chapters shifted into his additions, the mind under C. Holloway—the air seemed to thin. The words weren't mine anymore. They were colder, crueler. Detached.

Each line read like a confession written by someone who had been inside the moment, not describing it—living it.

She laughed, unaware that night was already closing its fist. The air was still, the world holding its breath. When the laughter stopped, so did everything else.

I froze. I remembered that line. I'd written the first half in an early draft, years ago. But not like that.

The rest of the paragraph twisted my voice into something unrecognizable, a whisper with teeth.

She stumbled, breath ragged, every step a prayer. He followed, silent. Close enough to feel the cold of his presence, but far enough to hope it was imagination. The steel waited, patient. Then the world went black, and her scream became someone else's thought.

The words throbbed in my mind, rhythmic as a heartbeat. I flipped through the pages faster, drawn deeper with every turn.

Somewhere near three a.m., I stopped at a passage that felt like a mirror cracking.

He told himself it wasn't him. That the shadows moved on their own. But the truth was simpler: he opened the door and never closed it again.

Something tightened inside me. My fingertips were numb. I could feel sweat pooling at the base of my neck. The lines on the page started to blur, not from exhaustion, from recognition.

This wasn't fiction anymore.

It was evidence.

My breath caught mid-inhale.

I started to remember.

***

It started as a faint whisper, barely more than a breath in the heavy silence, my mom's voice echoing inside my head, soft but steady. *"Sometimes... when you can't see the path, you have to trust that He's lighting the way."* Her words floated like a fragile flame flickering in the dark.

I wasn't sure if she said it to me or if it was a prayer she repeated to herself, it was a thread of hope she clung to in the suffocating quiet of our house.

Mom held onto faith like it was a lifeline when Dad's drinking took over everything. The smell of stale beer mixed with tension that seemed to seep into the walls. I never understood why she stayed, why she believed. But she said church was our refuge, our little escape from the storm.

And then the calm shattered like glass.

Her screams tore through my memory like jagged knives, raw and ragged. The air felt thick and metallic, the stench of fear and blood heavy in my nostrils. I saw it all again. The way Dad's anger filled the room, how he didn't know I was watching. I was just twelve, frozen in a shadowed corner, heart pounding so loud it drowned out everything else.

She didn't even see it coming, tearing a knife through her like she was nothing. The cold gleam of the blade flashed under the harsh light, slicing through the air repeatedly, relentlessly. The sound… wet, choking, desperate. It filled the room, swallowing her voice whole.

How could He take her from me?

She loved Him with every part of her soul.

And I loved her with everything I had.

But I was too scared. Too powerless to stop it. I just watched, trembling, unable to move.

No... make it stop.

The memories crashed over me like a wave; the weight of years I'd buried deep inside me. My knees buckled and I stumbled toward the bathroom, heart hammering like a drum.

I caught my reflection in the mirror. Eyes wild, jaw clenched, but my gaze was sharp, haunted. My mind felt like it was burning from the inside out, each memory like a hot coal searing through my skull. I didn't want to remember. I didn't want to feel this crushing weight.

Then, a voice. A faint, sinister whisper, barely audible but unmistakably there, crawling beneath my skin like ice.

If you listened to me more, you wouldn't have to feel this way.

What? Listen to who?

The voice was mine, yet it wasn't. It slithered through my thoughts, detached and demanding.

Desperate to silence the chaos, to escape the flood of memories and pain, I let the voice consume me. The edges of the room blurred and darkened. My legs weakened, and the world slipped away as I blacked out again.

***

The room tilted and faded away, swallowing Nick's senses whole. His heartbeat slows, his breath falters. His trembling hands drop uselessly to his sides. The light behind his eyes flickers and dies.

And I take the wheel.

I'm the shadow lurking in the corners of his mind, the fire beneath the ashes.

Where Nick is unsure, I am certain. Where he hesitates, I strike. I don't waste time with doubts or second guesses. I move with precision, every thought like a blade slicing through hesitation.

Nick wants to forget. I help him forget. His memories are nothing but rusted chains, and I cut them loose without a second thought. To me, they're useless, dead weight—trash.

His body obeys, but his mind is a prisoner, trapped behind a veil I control. Nick fades further, swallowed by the dark that I command.

I'm Clay.

Nicks too weak. But it's my turn with this body again.

For now, I go to the room and sit in the chair, fingers tapping the desk while the laptop screen glows in the dark.

I checked the sales dashboard. *Not Alone* is climbing again. Just like I knew it would. The royalties always come through, steady as a drip. I make sure Nick gets them, make sure he sees how much I've made for us. His fiction keeps him fed, keeps him steady.

The city house presses in around me and it's too loud, too cramped. I miss the lake house. My lake house. Bought it years ago while Nick was staring into the void, too numb to notice the paperwork sliding across the realtor's desk. He's never paying attention to what I do when he's too busy shutting down.

I close the laptop, letting the light fade. We'll go back there soon. That's where the real work happens. That's where I don't have to hide.

Suddenly, the shrill buzz of a phone shattered the silence, piercing through the fog of my return. I stretched; muscles stiff from being trapped in shadows and moved towards the source of the noise.

The phone screen lit up: Lucy. Her name blinking with a message that stirred something unexpected inside me.

"Good morning, Nick. It was nice seeing you, when do you want to hang out?" A heart emoji followed, soft and sincere.

My lips curl. Well, well… isn't she eager. She thinks she's just talking to him.

That's perfect.

I type a quick reply: *"It was nice seeing you too. How about dinner at 7? I'll pick you up after you close the bookstore."*

No flair, no emotion, just enough to lock it in. She'll think it's Nick being polite.

I lean back, letting Nick's body settle into the motions. I don't linger. Soon enough, he'll feel the consequences, and I'll be ready when he crumbles.

***

I wake up to the persistent buzz on my phone. Blinking against the light of the screen, I squint at Lucy's message: *"Looking forward to dinner tonight!"*

I frowned, pulse picking up. Did I… agree to this? Reading the messages. My head aches, muscles sore, memories blurred. The night before

47

feels like a foggy dream, one where I wasn't fully myself.

I text back, *"Great, see you later."*

Shoving my phone into my pocket, I muttered, "Great. How did this even happen?" But there's no time to dwell, Lucy will be waiting, and I can't let her see me falter.

I sank into the chair at the café; phone pressed to my ear. The line hummed for a moment before a calm, deliberate voice cut through.

"Nick," she said. "I've gone through your new manuscript. Dystopian, again. Robots, rebellion, freedom... it's competent. But it's missing tension. The stakes aren't high enough. The danger doesn't feel real."

I frowned. "Danger... for the characters?"

"Yes," Betty insisted. "Readers want to feel fear, desperation, obsession. They want the edge of unpredictability. Right now, it's too safe. Safe doesn't hook anyone."

I traced the rim of my coffee cup, uneasy. "I thought creating the world was the risk. The story should feel dangerous enough on its own."

Her laugh was quiet, teasing, just enough to unsettle me.

"Sometimes the best stories come from knowing the darkness intimately. From feeling it. Let your characters take the fall. Let them live the chaos so your readers can't look away."

I swallowed, my fingers firm around the cup.

"I... I'll see what I can do."

"Good," she said. "Keep at it. I want to see revisions soon."

The line went dead. I set the phone down and ran a hand through my hair. The café was quiet around me, but my mind was buzzing. There was work to do, edits to make, ideas forming faster than I could capture them.

I glanced at the clock. Dinner. Right. I had plans tonight. Folding my jacket over my arm, I stepped out into the evening air, the sun dipping low and the streets alive with the hum of cars. Lucy was waiting.

***

I pick Lucy up from the bookstore and drive us to a quiet little restaurant downtown. The lighting's soft, the smell of fresh bread and herbs filling the air. She talks about a new shipment they just received, but I can tell she's holding something back.

"Nick... I know this isn't easy," she says carefully, "but... maybe we should talk about C. Holloway."

"We can let Adam manage it. That's his job," I replied, trying to sound casual.

A low murmur of other diners' drifts around us, punctuated by the clink of glassware. A candle flickers between us, throwing soft lights across her face as she sets her fork down and leans in.

She takes a deep breath. "I don't know exactly... but the books... Some of the details are unsettlingly precise. You've probably read them and felt it too—like they're more than just stories. I guess I just worry about what that means. And about you."

I swallowed hard, my anxiety coiling. Something in the back of my mind whispered: *Feel it. Let it sink in. Don't flinch. Ask her what she knows.*

"I... I know," I said, voice steadier than I feel. "So... tell me what you think."

Her words come slower now, careful. "I don't know everything. But reading them... it just doesn't feel like normal fiction. The stories, the characters, the events—they line up with...

things that happened. Maybe it's coincidence. Maybe it isn't. But I worry."

Something tightened in my gut. Not fear exactly, but something heavier: fascination, dread, curiosity. A shadowy voice murmurs again: *Pay attention. Let it get under your skin. You know you want to hear more.*

"Anything else worrying you?" I asked, my voice low.

She paused, frowning. "It… it's different. I can't put my finger on it, but Holloway's writing is brilliant—the way he builds the story, the characters, the suspense… It's impressive. But the details, the little things he includes… they're just… creepy. Like they're pointing at something. I've barely started the last one. He just released it last month, but it already gives me chills."

I leaned back, letting the words settle.

"You've got a sharp eye. You should be working with Adam."

Her eyes flicked to mine, calm but watchful.

"Maybe. But right now… I'm just trying to make sure you're okay. This isn't easy to manage, and I want you to be careful."

Lucy stirred her drink and gave me a small, curious smile. "So anyways... how are you doing?"

I ran a hand over my face and sighed. "Honestly? Stressed. I had a brief meeting on the phone with Betty, from the publishing house. She... wasn't thrilled with the last manuscript I sent."

She raised an eyebrow, leaning a little closer.

"Not thrilled? That sounds vague. What did she say?"

"Something about it being disconnected," I muttered, feeling the frustration pressing in my chest. "Like I didn't know what I was doing. It's hard not to take it personally. Every word feels like mine but also like it's... never enough."

Lucy reached over and lightly tapped my hand. "Hey, don't let her get to you. You're the one who writes the story, not her. That's what matters."

Lucy's calm confidence settled something in me. I let out a slow breath, letting a little of the tension slip away. "Thanks," I said quietly. "It's nice, having someone in my corner for once."

She smiled, tilting her head. "You always have someone in your corner. You just don't notice it sometimes."

***

After dinner, I drove her home to her house. The place looks almost exactly like I remember from years ago, the chipped fence, the porch light humming against the night. Everything feels frozen in time. She lingered at the door, giving me that same friendly smile.

"You know," she said, nudging me with her shoulder, "I almost canceled on you tonight."

I let a small smile slip out, "Really? Just because I forgot. That's cold."

She laughs, warm and easy. "Yeah, well... don't make me regret it."

"I'll try not to," I teased, keeping my tone light.

But underneath it, a quieter thought flickers: *Keep her close. Pay attention.*

"Goodnight, Nick," she said, like she's stepping back into a comfortable rhythm from years of knowing me. "See you around."

"Goodnight, Lucy," I replied. Warm enough to reassure her, but distant enough to keep my composure together.

***

As soon as I got home, the spiral started. I wanted to forget, to move on, but everything kept dragging me back. Every step forward felt like a hand pulling me under. If I kept digging, I'd find answers I didn't want, answers that could ruin me, drive everyone else away.

Lucy has always been good to you, hasn't she?

The thought slid in, too steady, too calm.

Air felt trapped in my lungs. Was that me? Or someone else speaking through me?

The words felt both foreign and familiar, like an echo of something I'd always known but never said. Unease crept up my spine, twisting with a strange comfort I didn't trust.

I glanced around the room, irrationally checking that I was alone. My eyes landed on the rosary half-buried under paper on my nightstand. My faith had withered over the years, but the beads still felt solid in my hand, grounding. I whispered a prayer I wasn't sure I believed, clinging to the comfort of the ritual as I drifted into sleep.

***

It's pitch black, with only a spotlight following me. No matter how far I walk, there's no end. I don't know how long I've been moving, but eventually, a reflection appears ahead of me. A mirror?

I get closer, my steps echoing into the emptiness, until I'm face to face with myself. I lift a hand; my reflection lifts a hand. I look left, then right. He mirrors me perfectly. Then—it stops.

Fear flashes across my face, but the reflection's mouth curls into a faint smirk.

Hello, Nick.

I freeze, my breath shallow, my pulse thrumming in my ears.

I try to turn away, to put distance between me and the thing in the glass. But as soon as I move, he's there again, blocking my path, close enough that I can see the gleam in his eyes.

Always turning your back when it gets hard.

I swallow, throat dry, words jammed somewhere between my chest and tongue. I try to move, but my body won't respond. My limbs feel heavy, trapped beneath a weight I can't lift. My lungs suffocating, like someone was pressing down from above. Every time I try to call out, no sound came.

The room stretches and warps, familiar yet wrong, the edges of the walls melting into shadows.

You think you can face me?

Clay whispers, voice echoing, distant but everywhere.

I want to scream, to run, to move, anything—but it's like my mind's awake and my body isn't. Time warps. Every second stretching into a nightmare.

The voice carries through the void, low and steady, vibrating in my skull.

You don't need to answer. Just listen. You've been listening for years anyway.

My knees are weak. I want to scream, to wake up, but nothing comes.

It feels better when you stop fighting, doesn't it?

The reflection leans closer, whisper-soft but cutting like a knife.

You can't get rid of me, Nick. You and I... we're the same breath.

I'm frozen, my whole body screaming to move, but I still can't.

His smile widens.

I've been carrying the things you won't. I've been the one stepping in when you can't. And I'm not going anywhere.

The spotlight narrows, shrinking until it covers only him. My skin crawls as the light abandons me, leaving me in the dark.

Lucy. Adam. Everyone. You keep pushing them away, but I won't. I keep them close. I protect them.

His eyes glint.

Without me, they'd already be gone.

"Stop," I whisper, barely able to breathe.

He leans in, voice dropping to a velvet hiss.

You can't get rid of me, Nick. I'm what you've always needed. And you're what I choose to wear.

I jolt awake, trying to catch my breath, the echo of his words sticking to me like cobwebs. My room is silent, but I swear the reflection is still watching from the dark corners.

three

I woke up and couldn't really remember my dream. Just bits and pieces. It felt more like a nightmare. All I could remember is walking through an endless void and having a conversation with myself, but I don't even know what we had talked about.

The first thing I noticed is the rosary resting in my hand, tangled between my fingers. I tried to remember, but the moment I reach for it, something black and slick slides over it. All that's left is his voice. My voice, but not me.

You can't get rid of me, Nick. I'm what you've always needed. And you're what I choose to wear.

It echoed in my skull, bouncing off the inside of my mind until I wanted to claw it out.

My pulse spiked. Panic gnawed at my ribs. What was that? Who was that?

Anxiety crept in, weight pressed in the pit of my stomach. I sat up, my fingers clutched the rosary as if it might anchor me to something real. Desperate for answers, I pulled out my laptop and started searching: What causes memory blackouts? Could this be a mental illness? Stress? Sleepwalking?

Every article I read offered plausible explanations like depression, dissociative disorders, and trauma. They made sense. But I wasn't convinced.

With the rosary still clutched in my hand, I typed into the search bar: "links to demonic possession". The results were sparse but enough to make my insides lurch.

I saw forum posts, stories of people having nightmares, strange blackouts, and unsettling behavior they couldn't explain.

One thread caught my eye: "Signs someone is possessed or being haunted."

I hesitated, then clicked the link. The words crawled across the screen: blackouts, unexplained violence, voices in the head.

I shook my head, trying to push the cold fear away. No. This is nonsense. It's got to be a medical explanation. But the blackouts, the voice in my mind... it doesn't add up.

I shuddered and closed the tab. Demonic possession? That's ridiculous, I told myself. I'm not crazy.

And yet… the rosary, the voice, the darkness I felt—it all gnawed at me. Maybe I am.

I stared down at the rosary again; the worn beads cool and smooth clutched tightly in my hand.

My mom's voice whispered in my mind, quoting the Bible, "The light shines in the darkness, but the darkness has not overcome it."

The words echoed softly, offering a soft thread of comfort, but it was quickly broken by the buzz of my phone. Adam. He asked if we're still on for tonight.

Clinging to a sense of normalcy, I checked the date, it's only the next morning. It felt like too much was happening all at once. I had a therapy appointment today, too. Maybe that's good, maybe it's what I need.

I replied quickly, promising to meet Adam at the bar later.

I slumped against the wall, the weight of everything crashing back. Relief, yes, but also a gnawing fear of what I couldn't remember, what might be lurking in the shadows of my mind.

I stepped into the shower, letting the warm water flow over me, hoping it could wash away the heaviness weighing on my chest.

I focused on the steady rhythm of the droplets hitting my skin, trying to drown out the thoughts that swirled in my mind.

I forced myself to act normally, to pretend nothing was wrong, pushing everything. Fear, confusion, doubt—I pushed it deep down where I couldn't ignore it.

But no matter how hard I tried, the noise inside wouldn't quiet completely.

***

Back in my therapist's office, the one with the weird abstract paintings that look like they're watching you, and the dim, muted light that feels too quiet. I sat down, trying to steady my racing heartbeat. The silence stretched between us like a thick fog. She looked at me kindly, waiting.

"How have you been since our last session?" she asked softly, her voice was calm but expectant.

Every muscle in my body was tense. I wanted to speak, to unload everything crashing inside me, but the words stuck in my throat. What if I say too much? What if she decides I'm too broken? The thought of being locked away in a mental institution or prison made my heart twist cold.

I swallowed hard, forcing a small, safe smile.

"I've been... okay. Same old, you know? Just trying to keep busy, keep my head up."

She nods, her eyes searching mine. "Sometimes 'okay' hides a lot. Anything in particular weighing on you?"

I hesitated, the urge to be honest wrestling with fear. My fingers curled snug in my lap. "Just stress, I guess. Writing, work, life. Nothing new."

She leaned forward a bit, gentle but persistent.

"Nick, it's okay to tell me what you're really feeling. This is a safe space."

I wanted to believe her. I wanted to tell her about the blackouts, the voice, the fear clawing at me every night. But the walls I've built are strong.

I shook my head, keeping my voice steady, "I know, but I think I'm managing."

She let out a soft sigh, a mixture of concern and understanding. "Managing can sometimes mean hiding pain, Nick. Remember, healing starts with facing the hard stuff, not running from it."

Dr. Ames leaned back, her eyes calm but probing. "Nick... can we talk about Claire for a moment?"

I tensed but didn't pull away. "Sure... what about her?"

"How have you been coping since… you know, her passing?" She spoke carefully, almost like she didn't want to break something fragile.

I exhaled, trying to keep my voice steady.

"I'm… okay. I think. I mean, it's been years. You learn to live with it."

"Years, yes," she said gently, "but I also notice you haven't… moved on in certain ways. Haven't dated anyone. Haven't really let yourself start over. I just want to check in; make sure you're not burying it too deep."

I looked away, clenching my hands in my lap.

"I… I'm not sure what moving on looks like. I loved her. I don't… I don't know if I can ever… you know." My voice caught. "I'm not avoiding life, I just… I don't know how to let someone else in."

Dr. Ames nodded, giving me space. "That's understandable. It's not about forgetting her, Nick. It's about giving yourself permission to keep living, even if it's hard."

I gave a small, almost imperceptible nod, swallowing hard. "Yeah… I think I get that."

Dr. Ames's gaze softened, but there was a weight behind it. "Have you thought of your mom lately?"

The words hit differently, harsher this time. Her words landed heavier than I expected. I could feel the weight crushing in my gut.

I wasn't ready to go there—not yet—but the question hung in the air, insistent. My jaw stiffened, and I looked away, focused on the faint scuff marks on her office floor instead of her eyes.

Have you thought of your mom lately?

Her question echoed in my mind snapped something in me.

"Why would I think about her?" I fired back, sharper than I meant to. My voice ricocheted off the walls, and even I flinched at the edge of it. "She's not here. Thinking about her doesn't fix anything. It's just... pointless."

I crossed my arms, leaning back like I'm trying to put distance between us, between the question and me. She tilted her head slightly, not rising to my tone, but I could feel her eyes on me, studying, dissecting.

My chest felt compressed. I know I'm overreacting, but I couldn't stop. "Besides, what's that got to do with anything I'm dealing with now? Don't tell me you're about to ask about my dad next." The words came out clipped, like I'm daring her to answer.

She didn't. She just let the silence stretch until it was suffocating.

Realizing I'd rather sit in silence, she says, "I'd say your response is saying more than you understand yourself. I can see you're not ready to talk about it, so we don't have to."

***

When the session ended, I stepped out into the hallway feeling more unsettled than relieved. The quiet here didn't feel safe, it felt watchful. Like shadows lingering just out of sight. After everything that's happened, what if this really is something darker? A demon, maybe. And if I dared say that aloud, it'd be the fastest ticket to a padded cell... or a cold one.

I shook the thought off as I stepped into the blinding, too-bright daylight outside and slid into my car.

Driving home, I deliberately avoided my usual route. I wasn't ready to face the weight of my own walls. Too many ghosts there, too many memories pressed down. The streets blurred past in a dull stream of buildings, houses, and empty sidewalks, each one just another reminder of everything I was trying to run from.

At a stop sign, my eyes caught something familiar: the old church my mom used to take me to. How had I ended up here? I hadn't meant to come this way. Was it a sign?

The church doors stood wide open, like an invitation or a command. I felt it tugging me forward.

Before I knew it, I was standing at the foot of those worn stone steps, staring up at the tall stained-glass windows, the late afternoon sunset casting fractured colors onto the cracked pavement. The place stirred something inside me, a fragile memory I tried hard to bury.

Before the floodgates could open, a voice came from behind me, soft but steady, "What troubles you, son?"

Startled, I turned slowly. The priest's eyes held a kindness that didn't judge, as if he saw the weight I carried. I wasn't ready to admit the truth, not yet.

"What makes you think something's wrong?" I asked, forcing a casual tone.

He smiled, gentle and knowing. "Believe it or not, unfamiliar faces show up around here for a reason. Usually because they're seeking salvation. 'Ask, and it will be given to you; seek, and you will find; knock, and it will be opened to you' (Matthew 7:7)".

The words hung in the air. I blurted out before I could stop myself, "I don't think I can be saved."

Without a word, the priest moved toward the confessional and slid inside, his presence calm and patient like he was waiting for me.

This was crazy. I didn't even know why I'd come here. But maybe... maybe it was worth trying.

***

My legs moved before my mind caught up. I pushed open the confessional door, stepped inside, and sat down, hoping, praying, that this might be the place where I found some kind of peace.

The small wooden booth creaked as I shifted in my seat. The wall between me and the priest gave me the illusion of privacy, though I knew he'd seen my face before I stepped in. My palms rested on my knees, damp and restless.

"This is all confidential, right?" My voice was quieter than I intended, almost swallowed by the muffled stillness of the church.

"The only ones here are you, me, and the Lord," the priest said, his tone warm, deliberate.

There was a pause, then his voice came again, softer, almost coaxing. "First, tell me, what is your relationship like with God?"

I stared at the shadowed lattice between us, "I stopped going to church a long time ago... since I was a kid." Shame colored my words, like I'd just admitted to a crime.

"Can you tell me what led you away from Him?" His voice held no judgment, only patient curiosity.

"That's not why I'm here," I said, more sharply than I meant to.

He didn't flinch, "Then tell me, son... why are you here?"

My breath caught, and I could feel the wood grain under my fingertips, grounding me. "Sometimes I black out," I began, the words scraping out of me. "And when I wake up... I don't remember anything."

Silence. He let it hang, not pushing, just waiting.

"Last night, I fell asleep praying, and I had a nightmare," I continued, my voice shaking despite my efforts to keep it steady. "And I feel like I haven't been myself in a while."

The air in the booth felt heavier and warmer.

"How long have you been experiencing this?" he asked, his voice deep with concern, so genuine it made me want to believe he wouldn't have me locked up in some padded room.

I looked down, though I knew he couldn't see me. "Some years," I admitted. "At first, it was just minutes... hours gone. Recently it's been days. I don't know what this is. I just want it to stop. It needs to stop."

His reply came low and steady, as if the words themselves were a shield, "Submit yourselves therefore to God. Resist the devil, and he will flee from you" (James 4:7).

The tension melted away in my chest. I didn't feel sane exactly, but I didn't feel entirely crazy either.

"Do you think I'm… being possessed?"

"I can't tell you if you're being possessed," he said after a pause. "But I would like to pray with you."

The faint scent of incense from earlier mass drifted in, making the booth feel more sacred, more watchful.

We bowed our heads together in silence, letting the words settle.

After the priest said his prayer for me, silence filled the room before he continued, "The choice will be yours. But remember, 'The light shines in the darkness, but the darkness has not overcome it.'"

The priest's words hung in the air, steady and sure. I blinked, the verse settling somewhere deep inside me, but a flicker of unease sparked. Why that one?

I brushed the thought away and thanked the priest for taking the time to help me. The weight of it, finally telling someone about the blackouts, felt strange. Not lighter exactly, but less suffocating.

***

The drive home blurred by. My head was too crowded to notice traffic lights or the way the sky bled into the evening.

I forgot all about meeting Adam at the bar until I was already stepping through my front door. Guilt tugged at me.

I shot him a quick message: *Sorry, couldn't make it tonight.*

I didn't have the energy to lie. He'd see right through me.

I ordered Chinese even though I didn't have too much of an appetite. The smell of fried rice and orange chicken filled the living room, but it only made my stomach turn. I put on a movie, something I'd seen before. Hoping the noise would drown out the storm in my head.

A knock broke through the dialogue on-screen. My heart was clenched. I checked the security feed. It was Adam, holding a six-pack. My car was in the driveway. If I didn't answer, he'd know something was wrong.

I opened the door, forcing a smile. "Hey. What brings you here?"

"Well, I know you don't like going out much, so I figured I'd bring the bar to you," he said, stepping past me without waiting for an invite.

"You know how to make yourself at home," I muttered, shutting the door.

He popped open two beers, handed me one, and flopped onto the couch. "We've known each other what... almost two decades? You hardly invite me over anymore. Then you bail on me tonight. So here I am."

"You know you're always welcome here," I said, meaning it, though tonight I'd wanted to be alone.

"Exactly. So, what's going on? Chinese and movie night by yourself? Lucy's not here, is she?" he said looking around the room.

"No Lucy. Just... stressed." The word felt too small for the truth.

"I get it," he said, sipping his beer. "How about video games? Been a while."

"Sure. Why not?"

As we played, something about the clack of buttons, the hum of the console, and the low light in the room made things feel almost normal again.

Adam had that effect—showing up right when the walls felt like they were closing in.

While we were playing, I said it like it was nothing, "I went to confession today."

Adam paused just long enough for me to notice, then went back to the game. "You haven't been to church in a while. What made you go?"

I kept my eyes on the screen, fingers moving, like if I didn't look at him it wouldn't sound as heavy.

"I don't know. My head's been... weighed down. Figured it couldn't hurt. Plus, I ran into the priest—felt rude just walking away."

Adam side-eyed me, like he knew there's more under the surface, but he didn't push.

The beer made the hours blur. By my third, my tongue loosened more than it should have. "I've been so stressed lately... feels like I'm going crazy. I think I might go spend time at my lake house."

Adam paused, his avatar pummeled on-screen. He turned to me, eyebrows pinched. "You have a lake house?"

The words hung between us like I'd just confessed to burying a body. I hadn't told anyone about it. It was bought years ago. I didn't remember buying it.

"Yeah," I said slowly, searching for the right version of the truth. "Just somewhere I go when I need to clear my head. Get away from town."

Adam stared at me a beat too long. Then, with a half-smile, "Huh. Guess I'm not invited then. So, it's not too far from here, is it?"

The alcohol must've been getting to me because now I'm answering his questions without hesitation.

"Yeah, it's a lake house out by Crescent Lakes."

Adam's expression didn't change, but his eyes sharpened, like he was filing the information away for later.

"And when did you purchase it?"

"A couple of years ago. It hasn't been that long," I said, hoping he would stop asking questions.

Adam sat there for a moment as if he were putting something together but not quite. He finally said, "Just be careful around there. I've had a handful of cases out that way. All of them solved except a few."

I chuckled, "I'll survive. It's just a lake house, not a haunted cabin."

Adam didn't laugh. "Some cases start out that way, you know."

I glanced at him. "Which ones?" I asked, aiming for casual but felt my stomach tighten.

He shook his head, "Doesn't matter. Just... be careful out there."

"Yeah," I said, forcing a shrug like it's nothing.

"I'll be fine."

"Well, it's getting late. I should probably get going before my wife yells at me for never being home." Adam's tone lit, cutting through the heaviness that had settled between us.

"Yeah, don't want her thinking I'm stealing you away from her," I joked.

He stepped toward the door and paused, looking at me—not with judgment, but with quiet concern.

"If you need anything, you can talk to me. I'm here for you."

His words hit harder than they should. Not because he cared, but because I've been lying to him, hiding from him.

"Yeah, I know, man. I'm here for you too." I forced a smile, patting his shoulder, trying to reassure him everything was fine. Even though it wasn't.

After Adam left, I stood there, lost in thought. I know I can trust him, but could I really tell him what's happening? The blackouts. The forgetting. Part of me wants to say something. The other part knows that if I did, I could end up behind bars. Locked away.

***

A voice slithered its way into my mind—smooth, cold, unmistakably his.

You think you can handle this on your own? That talking will save you?

I gritted my teeth, trying to shut him out.

"Leave me alone. I don't need you right now."

Need me? You're drowning, Nick. You're nothing without me.

The darkness creeps in at the edges of my vision, pulling me under.

***

Finally.

Silence. Not peace. A silence that hums, thick and heavy, with my breath. I'm back again.

Adam stepped back into the room, scooping his phone off the coffee table.

"Forgot my phone."

He froze. Our eyes locked, and I saw it, the tension in his jaw, the way his hand stilled mid-motion. He knew it wasn't Nick standing in front of him.

"Long time no talk, Detective Chaplin," I said, my tone almost... friendly.

"Clay." His voice came out slow, careful, like he was speaking to a cornered animal. "Quit writing these damn books!"

I smiled. "You figured it out a long time ago, Detective. But here's the question, how come you haven't turned me in?"

He didn't look impressed. "You need to let Nick out. Now."

I chuckled, low and menacing. "No 'how've you been'? Straight to business. You always were a buzzkill."

Adam took a step forward; eyes locked on mine.

"Nick, if you can hear me—"

I held my face taut. "Don't," I said.

"You need to fight him. This isn't you. You can fight—" Adam continued.

"Don't talk to him!" My voice came out sharper than I intended, and I felt the faint stir in the back of my mind.

Nick, curious.

Listening.

Adam's gaze flicked, just for a second, like he could see the movement behind my eyes. "Nick, you're stronger than you think—"

I slammed my palm against the wall beside his head, leaning in so close I could smell the faint trace of beer on his breath. "Stronger? He's pathetic without me. All I've done for him—for us. Without me, he's just a trembling little boy who can't even think about his mom or dad without falling apart."

Adam didn't flinch, "Then let him face it."

I smiled, slow and cruel. "You and I both know, if he ever truly remembered, he wouldn't survive the night. That's why I'm here. Nick is why I exist."

For an instant, we just stood there. He's staring into my eyes, while I'm wondering if I should end him right here. But no... there were bigger games to play.

Adam's jaw locked. "Then why the murders?"

I let my gaze linger on him, callous and unyielding. "Maybe... I make it easier for others to do what they want. Or maybe it's just... fun to watch how people react."

The flicker in his expression told me he knew Nick was coming back. I could feel it too. The pull, the scratching at the edges of my mind. He was crawling back, desperate to take control.

I can't do anything with Adam here, anyway. I'll let Nick have his body back, for now. More time for the rest of my plans to unfold. And when he realizes he blacked out right in front of Adam? That might eat him alive.

I threw Adam a slow, knowing smirk. "See you soon."

***

The darkness ripped away like someone yanking a curtain open. My lungs seized, drawing air too fast, my pulse hammered in my throat. Then the soft click of the door shutting closed. Was someone here? No... I must be losing it again.

Exhausted from the alcohol and the blackouts, I collapsed onto the couch, letting sleep claim me.

***

I woke up with a dull ache at the base of my skull, the kind that makes your thoughts feel like they're swimming through syrup. Sunlight cut through the blinds in pale strips, catching dust in the air. The clock read 9:42. Too late for a productive morning. Too early for the kind of exhaustion weighing me down.

Something was there, just beyond reach. Adam's voice. The sound of water. The creak of wood underfoot. I tried to pull it closer, but the harder I reached, the faster it slipped away.

I know I told Adam about the lake house, was he suspicious of me now?

By late morning, the house felt too still, the silence thick enough that I could hear my own heartbeat. I was staring at the blinking cursor on my laptop when a knock rattled the door.

I opened it to find Lucy standing there, framed in the pale light. Her hair caught the breeze, strands brushing across her cheek before she tucked them behind her ear. She held a paper bag close to her chest, the scent of warm bread and something garlicky escaping with every movement.

"I brought lunch," she said, her smile soft but bright, the kind that reached her eyes.

"You didn't have to—"

"I wanted to. Besides," she stepped past me, her shoulder brushing mine, "I still owe you."

"Thanks, I appreciate it." I say, still feeling out of it, trying to remember exactly what happened last night after Adam left.

"You, okay?" Lucy's voice snapped the thread of the memory.

I blinked, the image dissolving like fog in sunlight. "Yeah," I lied. My voice caught. "Guess I'm more tired than I thought." I tried forcing a smile.

She gave me a small smile and started unpacking lunch, talking about an art exhibit she wanted to see next week. I nodded in the right places, but I couldn't shake the feeling I got last night.

Keep her close. The familiar voice slithers into my head. The voice I keep listening to while trying to ignore at the same time.

***

The days afterwards blurred together. Lucy came by more often, sometimes with coffee, sometimes with dinner. We settled into a quiet rhythm: she'd read or write on the couch while I sat at my desk writing my dystopian fiction.

Adam texted now and then, just enough to remind me he was still there. I kept my replies short. Not being alone was something I probably just needed.

It felt almost normal. Almost.

This evening, Lucy was at the sink, humming a tune I didn't recognize. I caught my reflection in the dark kitchen window.

For a split second, it wasn't me. The smirk was harsher, the eyes colder, like whoever was looking back already knew something I didn't.

I blinked. My own face stared back.

But the thought that followed wasn't mine.

Take her somewhere quiet. Somewhere no one will bother you.

I pushed the thought away, but it lingers like a shadow at the edge of my mind. My eyes dropped back to my laptop, typing more words across the pages. I'm so close to finishing this book.

"Hey, Lucy," I said without looking up at first, the words slipped out as I typed. "Since I'm almost done, we should celebrate, do something fun together."

She perked up, a hint of excitement in her eyes.

"What do you have in mind?"

I finally glanced at her, trying to keep my voice casual. "What about a small getaway? I've been thinking about visiting my lake house soon. You should come with me."

"That does sound fun." She leaned against the counter, already considering it. "I'd have to find someone to cover the bookstore, though. Could we plan for... maybe next week?"

"Next weekend it is, then," I say, voice steady, though my pulse has picked up. Something about this feels... deliberate. Planned. And I have the sinking feeling I'm not entirely in control.

***

I can't shake the words from yesterday as I settle in at my desk the next morning. I'm halfway through a sentence in my book when a knock hits my door. I didn't even look up. "Come in," I called, expecting Lucy.

It's Adam.

"Hey, man. What's up?" I kept typing, but my eyes flicked to him. He's not smiling.

"I need to tell you something, Nick." His voice was low, heavy.

"What is it?" I asked, fingers still tapping keys.

He didn't hesitate.

"Your dad… he's released on parole."

My hands stopped. The air between us was suffocating. A mix of heat and blood rushed to my head so fast it made me lightheaded.

"How the hell was he let out already?" The words came out louder than I meant. "Why?"

Adam shifted his weight, watching me like he's measuring every movement for signs of something else. "I know you're upset, but—"

"Upset?" My voice was almost a laugh, but there's nothing funny about it. "He's a danger to society. Or did you forget what happened?"

"Did you?" Adam says, his eyes flickered with the kind of worry I've seen before, not just for me, but for what might come out.

"He's not going to listen to you."

The voice comes from behind Adam, low and familiar enough to freeze me mid-breath.

I knew that voice.

When my eyes locked on him, it's like my stomach dropped out from under me.

My dad stood in the doorway, smiling like we're old friends meeting for coffee. The light from the window catches on the edges of his face, making the lines deeper, his eyes brighter.

I glanced at Adam, betrayal cutting through my chest like glass. "What the hell is going on?"

"Nick… it's been so long." My dad stepped closer, hands out in a slow, placating gesture.

"Get out. You're not welcome here." My voice shook, more from rage than fear. "Adam, why did you bring him?"

Adam opened his mouth, but my dad cut him off, his tone soft, almost gentle. "Don't be mad at him. I asked him to take me here. I understand why you're upset. And I failed you back then… but we can fix this—"

"Fix what?" The unease constricted my lungs. "There's nothing to fix. You killed Mom and you deserve to rot in prison. If I had a choice, I wish you got the death penalty."

Adam's gaze narrowed slightly, but there's something unreadable in it. "Is that really how you remember it?"

For a split second, the room tilted, a wave of nausea swelled in my gut.

My dad shook his head with a sad smile.

"No, it's fine. Maybe this is best. I shouldn't have come here. I'm probably just making things worse."

Emotions surged like a flood I couldn't hold back. I didn't want to see my dad. He shouldn't be here; he should be in prison. My grip on myself is slipping, shadows curled at the edge of my mind. Adam and my dad exchanged a glance, they can see it happening.

"Sometimes… when you can't see the path, you have to trust that He's lighting the way," Dad said, his tone deliberate, knowing exactly which wound he's pressing. It hit like a match to dry kindling.

"How dare you," I snapped, my voice sharper than I intended. "Taking what Mom said and twisting it to make things better? You didn't even have faith. You were nothing but an abusive alcoholic—"

The door creaked open. Lucy stepped in, her brow furrowed. "What's going on? I'm sorry, I didn't know you had any company, wait, Mr. Smith?" Lucy looked at my dad in shock, then toward me, clearly confused.

"They were just leaving," I snapped, the silence stretching thick around us. Adam and my dad exchanged another glance and moved towards the door.

"I almost didn't recognize you." My dad rests a hand on Lucy's shoulder. "Take care of yourself, Lucy," he said quietly as they left.

I took a deep breath and let out a shaky sigh.

"He's... out on parole," I muttered, clenching my teeth as I looked away, trying to stop the pulse hammering in my chest. Silence hung heavily between us.

She reached out, tentatively, placing a hand near mine. "Nick... you don't have to go through this alone, you know."

I forced a small nod, not ready to meet her eyes.

"I know. Just... give me a minute."

The words hung in the air, unspoken things pressed down on both of us, and I can feel the weight of questions I'm not ready to answer yet.

four

After meeting with Nick, I can't stop wondering if I'm doing the right thing.

I met Nick Smith when we were fourteen, back when detention felt like the worst punishment life could hand us. I was the new kid in town, trying to disappear in the back row, but he was already there. His head bent over that damn notebook of his, scribbling like the world might end if he stopped.

Everyone else was killing time, staring at the clock, but not him. Something about that struck me. Maybe it was the quiet intensity in his eyes, or maybe I just knew even then that he was carrying something heavy.

Everyone in town knew his story. The tragedy that followed him like a shadow. His mom. His dad. The kind of whispers that traveled fast in high school hallways, turning pity into unwanted popularity. Nick hated it.

I could see it in the way his jaw tightened when people looked at him too long. He didn't want sympathy. He wanted normal.

Instead of bouncing around foster homes, Nick moved in with my parents for a while. From that moment, he wasn't just my friend. He was my brother.

But even back then, I noticed the cracks. The way he could vanish inside himself for days, then suddenly come back blunt, charming, magnetic, like nothing was wrong. How he could own a room one night and look hollow the next morning? I told myself it was stress, trauma, just the scars of a broken home.

We all carry something, right?

His social worker made him see a therapist, though Nick never talked often about it. I figured it was helping. He was functioning, surviving, even thriving in his own way. And no matter how much space he claimed to need, he and I were always side by side.

Throwing a ball, killing hours in silence, watching movies, grinding through video games, or him dragging me to parties I didn't want to go to. I'd never really wanted to go, but I'd never let him go alone either.

Nick always told me, "If I ever lose it, pull me back. Don't let me go too far."

A joke he'd say before doing something stupid. But looking back I wonder how far the truth went in that joke.

**

Nick was reckless; I was the one trying to keep him from going off the rails. I remember the day he almost ruined my future before it even started, lessons learned.

We were eighteen, still dumb kids trying to act cool. Somehow, he convinced me to lift things from a store, stuff we couldn't afford but thought we needed.

Nick was always good at persuasion.

We got caught.

I was terrified. So terrified that when the police officers started questioning us, I pissed my pants. As humiliating as it was, it ended up saving us. I told them their harassment made me do it. Somehow, they bought it and we walked out free.

That was Nick. Always in trouble. And me? Always pulling him out of it. If that's not friendship, I don't know what it is.

Sometimes I think that's what pushed me into becoming a detective. Watching him. Watching people. Trying to understand the invisible weight they carried. Trying, maybe foolishly, to fix anything I could.

But Nick changed during college. Slowly at first. Fewer parties, fewer bruises, fewer nights where I had to drag him out of trouble. He was careful now, cautious, almost deliberate in how he moved through the world. I told myself it was maturity, maybe even healing.

I let myself believe he was finally okay. That he was safe. I was wrong.

***

My first big case came in the dead heat of August 2019. We were called to Crescent Lakes—word was a body had been found along the shore. They gave me the case because I was new, because they wanted to see what I was made of.

The scene hit me like a punch. The lake shimmered like glass, still and suffocating, but the silence was all wrong.

The body was nothing like what I'd seen before. Not my first corpse, but my first murder. Limbs bent at angles they weren't meant to bend. Skin pale and slack.

Whoever had done it hadn't just killed her, they had dismantled her, piece by piece. It looked less like violence and more like… sloppy art. An impatient artist—no, an impatient killer who couldn't stop cutting even after there was nothing left to take.

We had reports of missing women, one of them being Nick's fiancée at the time, her name was Claire.

The DNA results matched and the autopsy report said she'd had several drinks. She was stabbed to death repeatedly, long after her lungs stopped drawing breath. Rage like that leaves fingerprints even if the killer wears gloves.

And it sounded familiar. Too familiar. The brutality reminded me of those old newspaper clippings about Nick's father, about how he'd carved up Nick's mom in a frenzy of rage.

***

I remember having to interrogate Nick. He didn't like it any more than I did, but I had a job to do. Questions had to be asked, lines drawn, distance enforced—even when it felt wrong.

We sat in the interrogation room, the fluorescent lights too bright, the air stale. My boss was there too. He didn't trust me alone with Nick, not after everything we'd been through together. I understood why. That didn't make it easier.

Nick answered every question.

Too easily.

At the time, I told myself it was shock. People cope differently. But looking back… that was Clay. I just didn't know his name yet.

Nick's voice was steady. His emotions controlled, measured, like he'd rehearsed them. He said the right things, at the right times. Grief, confusion, fear—displayed neatly, exactly how a distraught fiancé should behave.

But I knew Nick.

The Nick I knew would've broken. He would've blamed himself. He would've begged me to arrest him for not keeping Claire safe.

The man sitting across from me didn't do that.

And it helped in Nick's favor.

***

After we let him go, my captain pulled me aside.

"You really don't believe your friend could do this?"

I didn't hesitate. "No."

He studied me for a moment. "That kind of certainty can be dangerous."

"Or it can mean I know him."

"Sometimes," he said, "people aren't who they present themselves to be."

The implication landed harder than it should have.

"Nick isn't one of those people. You saw it yourself in the interrogation room, didn't you?" My voice came out sharper than I intended.

He set a hand on my shoulder. "I know this is hard. I just hope you're not wrong about him."

He gave me a faint smile, a small nudge, and walked away.

He never questioned me about Nick again—until, a year later, a book landed on my desk.

***

August Rush by C. Holloway.

I didn't read the whole thing myself, but my colleague did. He marked passages, underlined them, shoved the pages in my hands. His voice shook as he explained it: the protagonist, a killer. He stalks then kidnaps a woman, stabs her to death in a blind rage. The way it was written and polished, dressed in metaphor, made it sound like fiction. But the bones of it matched our case, almost word for word.

C. Holloway was a ghost. No address. No trail. Nothing. Like he already knew how to vanish.

My captain came up to me during a shift. "Isn't that friend of yours an author?"

I looked at him, the unease crawling up my spine.

"He writes dystopian fiction. Not whatever this is."

He didn't push it. Maybe he saw how offended I was that he'd even ask.

I remember telling Nick about *August Rush* and how it connected to Claire's case. His eyes darted, his voice cracked. He wasn't himself. And when I brought up the name C. Holloway… it was like I'd pulled a thread he didn't want me to see.

That was the first time I let myself think about it. The first time I looked at my best friend and wondered if he could be the monster I was hunting.

Dead bodies never made me flinch. But the idea of Nick as a murderer made me sick in a way no crime scene ever could.

I started digging. I started watching. And all roads led back to him. I needed answers.

***

I'll never forget the day I walked into that prison. Not just as a detective. Not just for a case. For him.

The prison loomed like a scar on the edge of town; a slab of gray concrete wrapped in razor wire that caught the sun like shattered glass.

Even after years on the force, places like this still made me uneasy—and back then, I was still considered a newcomer. Out here, the silence didn't just surround you. It pressed into your bones, rookie or not.

Inside, everything hummed. The fluorescent lights overhead, the cameras swiveling to follow me, the buzz and clang of heavy doors locking behind me one by one. The air smelled of bleach, pungent and chemical, but it couldn't mask the undercurrent of sweat and rust clinging to the walls.

I signed in as a visitor. No badge. No department name. Just a last name, a first name, and a box checked for personal visit. No one asked why. They never do.

A guard led me through a corridor of echoing footsteps, each steel door I passed nothing more than a number, a sliver of life locked away.

When we reached the visitation room, it felt less like a meeting space and more like a cage disguised with furniture. Other tables were already occupied, voices murmuring low, the scrape of chairs echoing off concrete walls. Plastic chairs. A metal table bolted to the floor.

When they brought him in, I knew instantly who he was. The resemblance to Nick was undeniable. His wrists rattled with chains as he sat across from me, the clink of metal punctuating the silence like a warning.

For a long moment, neither of us spoke. A laugh rose from somewhere behind me, cut short by a guard's bitter look. I studied the man who had shaped the boy I knew. Nick's father's eyes were cold, pale, and unblinking, and for the first time in my career, I understood why people said silence could be louder than words.

I leaned forward, my palms flat on the table's icy surface. "You're the reason he's like this," I wanted to say. Instead, the words caught in my throat. All I could do was hold his gaze and try not to let the weight of it crush me.

I don't even know what I was looking for. Answers, maybe. Closure, maybe. Or maybe just someone to hate on his behalf. But when I sat across from Nick's father, the man who destroyed his life, I didn't find what I expected.

He looked older than I imagined, creased skin, thinning hair but not weak. His posture was precise, his eyes steady, dissecting me as if I were the one on trial.

"And you are?" he said. No smile. No handshakes.

A guard paced the room's edge, close enough to see us, far enough not to listen.

I sat down, pulse kicking harder than I wanted to admit. "Chaplin—Detective Chaplin." I caught myself, lowered my voice. "Adam. I'm here because… Nick's my friend."

His face softened in a way that unsettled me. "Friend," he repeated, like he was tasting it. A smile touched his mouth, small, sincere. "I'm glad to hear my son isn't alone. That makes me happy."

Happy. That word rattled me. How could a man who killed his wife say that with a straight face? I wanted to snap back, to tell him exactly what I thought of his happiness, but I held it in.

"I'm not here to stir anything up," I said instead.

"Honestly, I don't know why I came. Maybe I thought I'd… yell at you. Tell you what you took from him. Ruined his life. But you're not what I expected."

His face turned into a grim line, eyes narrowing like I'd struck a nerve. "I ruined his life?" he asked quietly. He leaned forward, and the overhead light carved shadows across his face. "Some things aren't meant to be understood, Detective. They're meant to be carried. Quietly."

My mouth went dry. It was as if he knew why I was there.

He didn't stop.

"I know what Nick believes happened. And if believing it keeps him breathing, then you don't take that from him. You hear me?" His stare was sharp enough to pin me in place, like I was the one being warned.

Unease mounting in my chest. "What else is there to believe?" I asked, though my voice sounded smaller than I wanted.

His expression shifted, barely, but I saw it. A flicker of pity. Maybe relief. He didn't answer.

"Look after him," he said instead, his voice heavy now, final. "If you're his friend, then look after him. Don't let him dig where he shouldn't."

That was it. That was all he gave me.

By the time the gates clanged shut behind me, I was shaking with the urge to turn back and punch him in the face. But I didn't. There was a conversation to be had for another day.

I tried piecing the puzzle together, but every trail led to a place where I couldn't follow—toward him. And I couldn't let myself believe that. Not Nick. Never Nick. So, I let the case go cold.

***

It's rare that Nick and I fight. We usually set our differences aside, pretending the tension isn't there. But this time, it was different. I knew I had crossed a line, and I owed him an apology. I grabbed a six-pack and a pizza, hoping the familiar ritual might ease the weight between us.

By the time I knocked on his door, the evening light was fading, spilling soft gold across the porch.

He answered with that neutral expression he perfected, unreadable and calm. Still, the fact he opened the door was a good sign.

I stepped inside, setting the pizza box and beers on the kitchen counter. I cracked two open, handing him one, and took a sip of mine. The silence hung heavily in the air, punctuated only by the sound of what was on TV. I didn't know what to say.

Finally, Nick spoke. His voice was calm, almost detached, but the edge of suspicion was there.

"Why did you bring my dad here?"

I braced myself. I'd hoped he might let it slide, but I knew why he clung to it.

"That? That was my mistake. I wasn't thinking," I said, leaving out the half-truth. I wanted all three of us to talk, for them to reconnect. It might have been selfish, but I thought it would help him. Help him face his past, but he's not ready.

He didn't respond. I didn't push.

Instead, I grabbed plates and took slices of pizza, sliding one across the table to him. The warm smell filled the small dining room, mingling with the faint scent of brewing coffee left from the morning. I waited, watching him, wondering if he'd sit.

Finally, he did, across from me. That's when my eyes caught the book on the edge of the table, *Stay*

Awake by C. Holloway. A familiar panic curled in my gut. Nick had told me before he hadn't read too much of the books; I wasn't sure what to make of this.

"You start reading C. Holloway's books?" I asked, trying to keep my voice casual, but the unease slipped through.

He glanced at the book, then back at me, his expression calm but careful. "I started reading them," Nick said. "At first, it was just curiosity. My publisher has been on me to spice things up a bit—push darker territory."

He looked down, thumb tracing the edge of the cover. "I figured reading outside my comfort zone might help. See how other writers manage tension."

A pause.

"Somewhere along the way, it stopped being about inspiration. I thought maybe if I kept reading, things would... settle." He shrugged faintly. "Or they wouldn't. But at least I can say I tried."

I hesitated, weighing my words. Anytime I mentioned C. Holloway, something shifted in him, a flicker, a tightening of the jaw, a shadow passing over his eyes.

"Never thought I'd hear you say that. So... What's your opinion on this C. Holloway guy?" I asked carefully, trying not to push too far.

Nick paused, looking down at the book. His fingers traced the edge of the cover almost absently, and for a moment I saw the boy I'd known, the one who scribbled endlessly in his notebook.

But the warmth was gone. He looked up at me, eyes steady, voice quiet but controlled.

"He tells stories." He said, almost neutral, but there was a bitterness underneath, like steel wrapped in silk. "Stories that make you think. Sometimes about things you'd rather not think about."

He shifted in his chair, his gaze settling on the window instead of me. "I don't know if I like him… or if I should. But it makes you think about the things people are capable of. About… what's really out there."

The room felt colder for a moment, even with the faint hum of the air conditioning and the warm sunlight spilling through the window.

I took a deep breath, trying to steady myself.

"It's just a book, Nick. Fiction," I said softly, though even I knew some of it hit too close to home.

He looked at me then, eyes intense and unreadable. "Maybe. But sometimes, fiction isn't as far off as we like to think."

I nodded, letting the silence stretch between us, hoping that the small step of sitting together, sharing a beer and a pizza, was enough to start mending the rift. For now, that had to be enough.

The air between us thickened, heavy with unspoken truths. I sipped my beer, unsure how to navigate the pressure. But one thing was clear: the moment we could relax, really relax, was still a long way off.

I dropped the C. Holloway stuff. Right now, I needed to reach my friend. Tension coiling in my torso, words spilling before I could think.

"Remember that night, after you started staying with us… you were telling me about your dad. I've never seen you that upset before.

I could still see your hands shaking. I didn't know what to do or what to say, so we just got in the car and drove.

We blasted music with the windows down, letting the wind drown everything out.

And when we got to the lake, we sat on the shore and started skipping rocks. You hurled them like you were trying to shatter the whole lake. I've never seen you throw that hard.

Man, those were the days."

***

Nick's face shifted, the strain easing as a real smile tugged at his lips. His eyes softened, like the memory pulled him somewhere safer. For a second, the weight he carried seemed lighter.

"How could I forget that?" he said, his voice warming. "Remember when your parents took us out to the cabin—"

"The bat!" We both shouted at the same time, laughter breaking between us.

Nick shook his head, grinning wide. "We had no idea how it got in there, but when it swooped by your face, you screamed like a little kid." He broke into laughter and took another sip of his beer.

"No way. That was you," I shot back, laughing too.

Truth was, we both screamed that night.

"And the look on your mom's face when she ran in," Nick added between laughs. "You were wrapped in a blanket like some kind of burrito, trying to swat it away with one arm sticking out. You were—"

I cut him off, "Afraid of getting rabies." I added, continuing to laugh.

I laughed so hard my stomach hurt. "You were on the floor, rolling. You made fun of me for days after that."

Nick's laughter lingered, bright and alive, and for a moment it felt like we were those kids again—safe, unbroken, the world no bigger than a lake and a cabin.

We spent the rest of the evening trading stories and laughter, dredging up memories that had been buried for years. For the first time in a long time, Nick looked like himself again—his smile was easy, his laugh unguarded, the jagged edges of grief and anger dulled by the glow of nostalgia.

When I finally stood to leave, the night had settled in around the house, quiet and still. Nick walked me to the door, clapped a hand on my shoulder, and told me not to be a stranger. I promised I wouldn't, and the door closed behind me with a soft click.

***

The drive home was calm, almost peaceful. My chest felt lighter, like I'd finally set down a weight I hadn't even realized I'd been carrying.

But the moment I stepped inside my house, the feeling slipped away.

Nick was reading C. Holloway's books.

The thought settled in my gut, heavy and unwelcome. I couldn't shake it. Was it helping him heal—or feeding something that never really went away?

I tossed and turned, sleep creeping in but never staying, until the sheets felt suffocating. Eventually, instead of waking my wife with restless sighs, I slipped out of bed and padded down the hall.

My office is the only place I can think, the only place I can let the thoughts breathe without hurting anyone else.

The case file sat where I'd left it, but it felt like it had been waiting for me.

The night *Stay Awake* hit the shelves in 2022, a colleague of mine tore through it in one sitting. The next day, his face was pale, voice sharp with disgust. He said the violence in the book was more than what he wanted to read, it was intimate. Too intimate.

We combed through old files, cold cases, anything that might have matched the details. Nothing fits. At least not at first.

Then months after the book had been released, we got the call to Crescent Lakes.

Another body.

A missing person.

***

Even now, I can see the way the mist hung low over the shoreline that night, the water black and still like it was holding its breath.

The woman's body was crumpled near the reeds, her clothes torn, her skin shredded. Mauled. That was the only word for it.

At first glance, it looked like a bear had gotten to her, tearing with a kind of rage that was almost human.

But the coroner was baffled, no bite marks, no animal prints, no signs of struggle in the dirt. Just carnage.

And unlike the last case, this wasn't sloppy. It only looked that way.

The more I studied it, the more I realized this was precise. Almost deliberate.

The murder happened somewhere else, but her body was left lying there, displayed. I stared at it for so long it became hard to look away.

And then I remembered Holloway's words.

She stumbled through the woods; her voice lost to the dark. When they found her at the lake's edge, she was hardly recognizable. The water lapped at her feet as though trying to claim what was left. No one could say what had done it. The world would only whisper: monster.

Too close. Too specific. And yet, the crime scene and the pages never lined up exactly.

Her body had been found by the lake, just like the book said but the description of the victim didn't match, except her personality. Details were off, skewed, almost as if someone wanted it to look similar, but not identical.

And that was what unsettled me most.

Because similarities that close weren't coincidence. But differences that deliberate… those felt like misdirection.

We wanted to investigate C. Holloway, to peel back the mask and see who was really behind those words. But every trail went nowhere. The royalty checks led us into a maze of shell accounts and dead-end addresses, paper ghosts designed to vanish as soon as you touched them.

Whoever Holloway was, he knew how to stay hidden.

And still, I couldn't bring myself to follow the path that seemed most obvious.

Nick.

***

Unfortunately, the woman was one of Nick's fans. Her shelves sagged under the weight of the six novels he had released by then, most signed in his hand—reminders of every time she'd stood in line to see him.

Jessica never missed a signing, never stopped writing to him. But her devotion wasn't his alone.

Buried among her messages weren't just letters to other authors, letters to another name, one that twists the story darker: C. Holloway.

Every time the pieces started to align—his late nights, his haunted look, the way he flinches at certain headlines, his weekends out of town, I forced myself to look away. To doubt the evidence instead of him.

Because how could he have done it? The less I knew, the better it was.

I logged the interview the way I logged a hundred others—voluntary, procedural, another detective sitting quietly in the corner. On paper, it looked routine.

Nick, or at least the person in front of me, slumped into his chair in a way that seemed natural, tired but measured. His hands folded neatly on the table. Calm. Too calm, maybe. The Nick I knew would have filled silence with words. This one let it sit between us.

"You knew her," I said.

"She... she was a reader," he said softly. There was a flicker in his eyes, a pause that carried sadness, just enough that I believed it. Nick would've carried some grief like that. Whoever this was, had learned it well.

"You met her?" I asked.

"Yes. At my book signings," he said, voice careful.

"How many?"

He hesitated—just the faintest pause. Not a memory lapse, I realized, but a calculation.

"More than once."

Jessica had followed him from city to city. I knew that from the emails. Pages of them. Long messages dissecting his work, praising his mind, thanking him for writing characters that felt like her. Fan mail, technically. The kind writers are told to expect.

"She wrote to you," I said.

"Yes."

"Frequently?"

"Yeah… she really loved my work." He sounded genuinely sad this time, a small slump of the shoulders, a catch in his tone. But I noticed the little things that didn't match: the stillness of his hands, the precise way he measured every word, a micro-twitch of his jaw when I said her name. Not Nick. Not quite.

"She ever cross a line?"

"No, never. She was always friendly and had something nice to say."

The sadness in his tone was there, but the timing of it felt rehearsed. Human grief acted, but almost perfectly. Almost.

I watched his face for more—guilt, recognition—but it never surfaced. He was performing, perfectly layered, almost indistinguishable from Nick… except for those tiny, fleeting tells that only someone who truly knew him could see.

In front of me sat a file of photos from the scene. I hadn't put them between us. I didn't want to see how he'd react to her face.

Any other man would've been pressed harder. Meetings, repeated contact, obsession—it doesn't stay innocent for long.

I didn't push.

I wrote the report carefully: *Subject confirms multiple brief encounters with victim at public book signings. Ongoing fan correspondence consistent with professional author–reader interactions. No evidence of escalation. No probable cause for further action at this time.*

It was all true.

It just wasn't the whole story.

I closed the file and told myself I was protecting an innocent man from coincidence and circumstance.

Nick—or the version in front of me—stood to leave, paused at the door. For a moment, I thought he might say something. Confess. Crack.

He didn't.

I watched him walk out, carrying the calm with him.

And for the first time, I wondered if it wasn't Nick I was protecting at all—but whatever part of him knew exactly how to survive this. So, I let the suspicion rot in the back of my mind, unspoken, festering.

Later that day, my supervisor caught me in the hall.

"You really had him interviewed again?" he asked.

I nodded. "Standard procedure, since he knew her. Another detective observed the session."

He didn't push. Just a hard glance, like he was filing it away for later. Maybe he was right to. Sometimes doing the right thing isn't the easiest thing to explain.

And just like that, another case went cold.

Not all my cases go cold though.

Nowadays, I've solved enough to make it count. Most of the perps were sloppy, careless, the kind who thought wiping down a doorknob or ditching a weapon in the river was enough to erase their sins.

They always leave something behind. They always slip. And when they do, I'm there.

But the Holloway cases... they're different. No stray hair, no footprints, no mistakes. It's like chasing smoke, every time I think I've got it in my hands, it disappears.

That's the difference between the criminals I've put away and the shadow I'm chasing now. One bleeds their guilt all over the crime scene. The other writes it into fiction and vanishes.

And neither one is Nick.

***

I remember mentioning the case to him again a couple months later. We'd usually meet for a quick bite, but between the investigation and everything else, I'd put it off. Talking to him about it felt safe.

We were sitting at his kitchen table, beers in hand, the pizza long gone but the warmth of the evening still lingering. The room smelled faintly of hops and melted cheese, the kind of domestic comfort that made the world feel smaller, safer.

The case had been all over the news, and I knew he'd heard about it. He didn't ask me straight out, though. Nick never did. He just waited, quietly, and I could tell he already carried the weight before I even opened my mouth.

Still, I started talking, laying out the details, the gory specifics, the strange similarities to C. Holloway's book. The more I said, the heavier it felt. I kept glancing at him, looking for a reaction.

His shoulders tense.

His fingers drummed against the bottle, too fast, too tight.

He looked... cornered.

I wanted to stop. I should've stopped, but I didn't. The words kept spilling out, and I couldn't shake the thought that the darkness was crawling closer to him each time.

Then it happened, the light in his eyes dimmed, a shadow flickered across his face. And in that instant, I realized I wasn't just looking at Nick anymore.

Someone else was in the room with us.

"That sounds like a masterpiece," Nick said, his voice calm—too calm—carrying a weight I'd heard before. Precise. Measured. Detached.

I froze. For a split second, I wondered if I'd imagined it.

This was Nick, my friend, sitting across from me like nothing was wrong. And yet... the tone didn't belong to him.

"I wouldn't call it a masterpiece," I said carefully, watching his face, assessing the space between us.

My body stiffened. That focus—quiet, unwavering—was familiar. I'd seen it once before, under harsher lights, across a metal table. Back when every word had been chosen with intent, every emotion displayed just enough to be convincing.

Nick leaned back, a faint smirk tugging at his lips as his eyes narrowed on me.

"No," he said smoothly. "Maybe 'masterpiece' isn't the right word. But there's an art to it, isn't there? The planning. The execution. The way a story gets told... even in real life."

For a moment, I couldn't respond. All I could hear was that same voice from the interrogation room steadily, unshaken—wearing Nick's face.

I swallowed, forcing my mind to stay on the surface.

It was Nick.

It had to be.

I refused to let my imagination go deeper. But the thought lingered, crawling under my skin, settling in my core like a stone.

And that's when it hit me.

I wasn't just talking about the case with my best friend. I was staring into the mind of something else entirely.

Nick's expression didn't shift, but his tone did.

Calm.

Measured.

"Hello, Detective," he said, leaning back slightly, eyes glinting like he'd been waiting for this moment.

"Allow me to properly introduce myself."

I blinked, heart hammering, my beer forgotten on the counter. "What... what are you? Who are you? What have you done to Nick?" my voice cracked slightly, though I tried to mask it with anger.

He let out a soft, amused chuckle, tilting his head like he was studying me.

"I'm Clay. Any more questions, Detective?"

I gritted my teeth, leaning closer, every muscle in my body screaming for answers.

"Clay... is that the 'C' in C. Holloway? What does this mean for Nick?"

His smile didn't falter, but there was a glimmer of satisfaction, maybe even pride, in his eyes.

"It means you've been looking in the right places, Detective. Just not at the right face—you should feel honored to finally have figured it out.

How's it feel?

You solved the cases you've been looking for answers to. When it was in front of you the whole time—you knew but you turned your head away and that's useful to me. Thanks, Adam."

The room felt smaller, air thick with tension. My gut warped, but I couldn't look away. I realized, with a cold twist in my gut, I was facing the monster who had been hiding in plain sight.

"Dammit," I growled, slamming my fist against the table, the sharp echo bouncing off the walls.

He chuckled, a low, unsettling sound that made my stomach tighten.

"Oh, come on. I'm introducing myself, ready to answer your questions, and that's all you've got?"

"Let Nick go," I demanded, anger barely holding back panic.

He tilted his head, considering me.

"I don't keep him," he said. "I just... show up when he needs help." His mouth twitched, not quite a smile. "And he needs help more than he admits."

My lungs constricted. The room seemed smaller, shadows pressing in. Sweat prickled at the back of my neck.

At that moment, I didn't know what I was facing, a demon inhabiting my best friend, or a fractured part of Nick himself that had been hiding all these years.

Thoughts collided in my mind, chaotic but precise. I could feel panic clawing at my resolve, but one thing I knew: I had to pull Nick back, before he slipped entirely into whatever this was. Before it was too late.

I forced myself to take a slow breath, trying to calm the storm inside me.

My eyes locked onto him.

Not the thing in front of me, but the friend I knew. The one who'd laughed at my terrible jokes, who'd shared late-night pizza with me, who made me pull him out when things were bad. Our friendship, thicker than blood.

"Hey," I said, my voice low, steady, trying to anchor both of us. "You want a bread roll?"

I moved to the kitchen counter and pulled one out, slathering it with butter, like I did back then.

It was ridiculous, but bread had always been Nick's comfort food whenever he felt anxious. The simplicity of it grounded him, making him feel safe.

The smirk faltered, replaced by a flicker of recognition, or was it defiance? I didn't know. But I pressed on.

"I need you here, man," I said, reaching for his hand as I placed the bread roll in it.

"The guy who cursed at me for stealing the last slice of pizza. The guy who stayed up till 2 a.m. talking through every dumb high school prank. That guy is still in there. I know he is." I said, forcing a familiar smile.

He tilted his head, a shadow of Nick's old grin brushing the corner of his mouth, before the mask snapped back.

My insides weaved, panic and hope clashed.

"You always told me to pull you back," I muttered, voice breaking slightly.

"I'm trying, Nick. You just got to reach."

Silence stretched between us. The air felt thick, as if it was charged with electricity. My ribs rattled with each beat, every second dragging like a lifetime. And then a flicker of hesitation in his eyes. Just enough.

Desperate, I did the one thing I knew might work. I grabbed the bread and threw it at him, just like I did when we were teenagers.

Looking back, it was silly, but it always helped. He would focus on catching it, take a bite and feel grounded again. I could only hope it still worked.

He caught it.

He stared at the roll in his hand like it was a foreign object. For a long second, the room was silent except for the pounding in my chest. Then hesitation. His grip loosened. His lips twitched, almost like he might laugh, like he might be Nick again.

"Bread," he muttered, almost too soft to hear.

I swallowed hard, fighting the burn in my throat. "Yeah, eat the fucking bread rolls." I said trying to sound casual, just like when we were in high school.

He took a bite, chewing slowly. "So… what happened?" His brows knitted, eyes clouded with confusion.

"You just had a panic attack. No big deal," I lied, forcing a shrug.

I studied him for a long moment, searching for recognition, for anything. But there was nothing. The Nick I knew had no memory of what I'd just seen.

And that terrified me.

It wasn't just stress. It wasn't just Nick cracking under pressure. Something else was there—wearing his face, hijacking his voice.

I couldn't explain it, but I felt it deep in my bones: this wasn't all him.

I'd seen Nick panic before. I'd talked him down more than once. Even then, I'd known what to say. I'd know how to help.

This time, I didn't.

I didn't know where to start.

I didn't know how to reach him.

But I knew who I wanted to blame.

Nick's father.

Everything seemed to lead back to him.

five

Looking back, I remember the frustration chewing at me, relentless and unresolved. No matter how many times I circled the two cases, I kept landing on the same thought: this didn't start with Nick. The poison ran deeper.

It began with his father.

After finally meeting Clay, I went back.

Back to the prison.

Back to the man who'd shaped Nick into something dangerous.

I told myself I was calm. That I'd be careful. That I just wanted answers. But as I passed through those gates, all I felt was the heat of anger simmering in my chest.

When Nick's dad reached the table, he greeted me, "Adam," a warm smile spreading across his face.

I froze, thrown off balance. Why the hell was he happy to see me? The reaction crawled under my skin, and I hated the way it unsettled me.

The room buzzed with low voices, but I focused on him, letting the anger coil firm in my gut. I leaned forward, lowering my voice just enough to keep it between us. "Cut the crap," I said, careful, controlled. "You know you ruined Nick's life."

He didn't flinch. "Did you just come here to yell at me?"

I clenched my jaw.

"I didn't think so." His voice softened, almost parental. "Is Nick okay?" His eyes searched mine with concern that made me uneasy.

"Nick's fine," I snapped, though the way he asked, the way he meant it bothered me. Especially coming from the man who killed his wife.

"You wouldn't be here again if he was fine," he said simply. "What's going on with my boy?"

For a moment, I couldn't answer. Didn't know how. The words knotted in my throat, and whatever expression flickered across my face must've been enough. Because his gaze darkened with recognition.

"So, you've noticed."

His tone dropped, heavy with disappointment.

"The changes in Nick."

The room shrank around me. For the first time in a long time, I felt exposed, like someone was reading me instead of the other way around.

"I was hoping this day wouldn't come," he murmured, almost to himself.

Then his eyes locked on mine, steady and unblinking. "But you're chasing answers you're not ready to face."

His eyes softened in a way that unsettled me. It wasn't the look of a killer; it was the look of a father.

A father worried about his son.

"You think I don't know what I've done?" His voice was low, calm, almost mournful.

"Nick will never be free of me. I gave him life, and I ruined it in the same breath. I carry that every day here. But what you don't understand, Adam…"

He leaned forward, elbows resting on the table, his cuffed hands clinking against the metal.

"…is that I would still carry that weight for him. I already have."

I frowned, the words scratching at something I couldn't quite place.

"What the hell are you talking about?"

He smiled faintly, sad and resigned, his voice low enough to disappear into the room.

"You think I went down for what happened that night because the truth came out? No. I went down because I let it."

He held my gaze.

"Because that was the only way Nick could have a chance at a life. If someone had to be the monster in his story, I chose me."

Heat surged through me. My throat constricted, caught between anger and confusion. I kept my voice low, "So now you're claiming you took the fall for him?"

He shook his head. "Not for him. Because of him. There's a difference."

His gaze met mine, unwavering.

"You've seen it, haven't you?" he said, barely above a murmur. "The way something flickers behind his eyes. Like a shadow slipping past the light. You think you're chasing a ghost. But what you're really chasing…"

He let the words hang.

"…you already know."

The air in the room shifted. Heavy. Claustrophobic.

I leaned back in my chair, the scrape of metal too loud in the space. Conversations hummed nearby— low, indistinct—close enough that I had to measure every word.

I kept my voice even. Controlled. "You're full of shit."

He didn't argue. Didn't react at all. He simply leaned back, folding his hands, as if we'd reached the end of something he'd known all along.

The lighting carved his face in half, one side sharp, the other swallowed by shadow.

"Denial, I understand. But when it doesn't stop staring you in the face, you know where to find me."

I felt a chill creep up my spine and for the first time, the calm in his tone felt like a warning.

I left with his words echoing in my mind. I didn't fully understand what he was saying, yet.

***

Ever since that second meeting with Nick's dad and meeting Clay, everything shifted.

I started second-guessing myself, doubting my own mind. I buried myself in whatever cases came up, kept in touch with Nick like I knew nothing. I figured as long as I stayed close, I could prevent C. Holloway from writing again.

But the conversation with his father wouldn't leave me. It played on repeat, gnawing at me while I tried to piece things together. Was Nick's dad misunderstood, was he telling the truth?

There was one thing I knew he hadn't lied about, Nick's other side.

The way he spoke about it almost made me believe we were dealing with something supernatural, some demon wearing Nick's skin. But the deeper I dug into his past, the clearer it became this was something different.

Nick didn't know I had met with his father. He didn't know about the conversations we'd had. And to this day, I don't think he knows I've met Clay either.

I remember pulling up old files from his father's arrest, digging into every scrap of information I could find about their family.

Nick had told me bits before, his dad, an abusive alcoholic; his mom, a gentle churchgoer who tried to hold it all together. But on paper, the story was darker.

I dug deeper and found records I hadn't expected, calls made against Nick's mom. Neighbors reporting screaming, suspected domestic abuse. She was always intoxicated, always the one yelling. His dad, it seemed, was the one holding things together. Protecting Nick.

There was even a letter from someone at their church, insisting Nick's father could never have been guilty. They swore he cared for his son, took him to service every Sunday, and never missed mass even when his wife stopped going.

I couldn't believe what I was reading. It was the opposite of everything Nick had told me.

For a moment, I felt betrayed, like he'd lied to me outright. But that thought slipped away the second I remembered Clay.

That's when I started digging into disorders, memory loss, dissociation. Trying to make sense of it—to find an explanation for my friend.

My desk looked the same as it had back then—papers scattered everywhere, the air stale from too many late nights. Police reports. Psychology journals I had no business reading. Case notes scribbled into the margins.

I wasn't a doctor. I was just desperate to make sense of him.

The word kept coming up over and over again: dissociation. A defense mechanism. A mind splitting itself to survive.

I read about memory gaps, blackouts, entire stretches of life that vanished like smoke. I read about alternate personalities—alters—each one carrying the weight the original couldn't bear. Some were protectors. Some were violent. Some were gentle. Some were children, frozen in time. All were just trying to live a normal life.

I even went down a rabbit hole about demons—ancient ones, modern ones, the kind people blamed when science failed them.

The more I read, the more Nick's story made sense… and the less it made sense at the same time.

Had he lied to me? Or had he really believed what he told me? Maybe he hadn't been protecting himself from me at all. Maybe he'd been protecting himself from himself.

And the worst thought was the one I couldn't shake. If Clay was real—if he had always been real—how much of Nick's life had been stolen by someone else wearing his face?

After about a month of research and sleepless nights, I reached a conclusion. I didn't want Nick behind bars. I wanted him to feel normal, to live free from the shadow he doesn't want to acknowledge is there. Maybe it was the same thing his father had tried once, in his own way.

***

I found myself driving back to the prison, hating that I knew the turns by heart now.

The visitation room was already full when I walked in. Families clustered around tables, voices overlapping, grief and routine sharing the same air. I took the empty chair at the far end, back against the wall. It felt like the safest place to sit.

They brought him in a few minutes later. His eyes scanned the room once before finding me. That focus calm again. He sat across from me, close enough that we didn't have to raise our voices.

"Adam," he said quietly. "I wondered how long it would take."

"I'm not here as a detective," I said, keeping my voice low, careful. "I'm here because I don't know what else to do."

Something in his expression shifted, not surprise, but interest.

"What happened?" he asked.

I hesitated. Around us, conversations rose and fell, laughter too loud in one corner, someone crying softly in another. It gave us cover.

"There have been a couple of cases," I said. "Things that circle back to Nick. I told myself it was coincidence. I needed it to be."

His jaw tightened. His gaze dropped for half a second.

"Clay," he whispered.

The name landed heavy between us. Not a question. Recognition.

My pulse thudded.

"So, you believe me."

"I always did." He met my eyes. "The question is whether you understand what you're dealing with."

"I understand enough to be even more worried," I said. "He's trying. He's in therapy. But I can't keep pretending I don't see it."

"You can't help him alone," he said. "And not if you keep thinking Nick is the problem."

I swallowed. "Then what is Clay?"

He leaned back slightly, casual to anyone watching. His voice barely carried.

"Clay isn't an accident," he said. "He was shaped."

"By what?"

"By us," he said. "His mother. Me." A pause.

"And by Nick himself."

The room felt stifling, the noise pressing in.

"I'll figure something out, old man" I said, forcing the words steady.

He studied me, then said softly, "Careful, Adam. Saving him might cost you more than you realize."

***

After leaving the prison, I buried myself in Nick's dad's records: sentencing papers, parole files, past complaints—twenty years to life, parole possible, but nothing simple.

In fact, he wasn't the monster I'd imagined. He visited Nick's school, a hardworking man and loving husband.

After Nick's mother's death, his dad sent letters from prison reminding Nick, he loved him... in small, human ways that shocked me. Eventually, Nick requested no contact with his dad.

His mother, on the other hand, had multiple records, proof that she had been unstable, unpredictable.

Against my better judgment, and every rule I was supposed to live by, I pushed for parole. I didn't forget anything. Didn't lie outright. I just nudged where I shouldn't have, convinced myself a little freedom might help him reconnect with Nick, maybe guide him back.

The parole went through. The reconnection didn't.

And here we are—still trying to untangle everything, still trying to make sense of the past and present. Still trying to protect Nick.

The crowd was oblivious to the storm in my head as the sun blazed down Main Street. I almost ran straight into her before I even recognized her.

"Lucy," I breathed, a little startled.

Her head tilted, brows knitting slightly, as if trying to place me.

"Sorry, do you have a second?" I asked, trying to sound casual even though my pulse had spiked.

Her expression softened at once. "Oh! Adam. Right. Sorry, I almost didn't recognize you." She laughed lightly, brushing a strand of hair from her face.

"You don't need to apologize." I forced a smile, "Well, I didn't imagine running into you today."

Her smile was easy, warm. "Nice to see you again. I hope you patched things up with Nick. You know, he got real upset seeing his dad again."

"Ya, I don't know what I was thinking. We had drinks the other night," I said, keeping my tone neutral. "Though I think he's got a lot on his mind lately."

Lucy nodded, listening attentively. "He's been busy writing, huh? He mentioned taking me to his lake house next weekend. Seems like he's finally getting time for himself."

I felt a twinge of protectiveness.

"Yeah… he's been pushing himself a lot lately. I guess I just worry sometimes."

She gave me a reassuring smile. "I get it. He's lucky to have someone looking out for him."

A soft ring from Lucy's bag breaks our conversation. She reaches for her phone to see who it is.

"Sorry, Adam, I need to take this call, I'll see you around."

I nod, "No problem, Lucy, see you."

As I walked away, I couldn't shake the feeling that I needed to keep an eye on Nick.

Lucy. Was she next? Had Clay already marked her, waiting to strike? Or worse—had she unknowingly welcomed him in?

The thought gnawed at me until I panicked.

There was only one person I could go to, the one person who'd understand the danger, even if he carried half the blame.

Nick's father.

***

I drove to the cheap motel where I'd set him up in off 13th Avenue, a place where the carpets were stained and the doors had been kicked in too many times, the neon vacancy sign buzzing like an insect.

I parked in the restaurant lot across the street, not daring to directly pull in. In this neighborhood, a detective's car was a spotlight no one wanted.

Walking down the block, I kept my head low, shoulders hunched. Addicts slouched against the walls, prostitutes leaned into car windows, everyone moving in their own orbit of survival. I didn't make eye contact. I didn't want to stand out.

When I knocked on the door, it opened a crack. The smell hit me first, stale smoke clinging to the walls, a faint hint of bleach that didn't quite mask the rot of decades-old mildew.

"Oh," his father said, surprised but not unwelcoming. "Didn't know you were coming by today. Come in."

I stepped inside, setting the bag of food I picked up for him on the table. He'd made the room his own in the way only ex-cons could, neat, orderly, everything folded or stacked like he didn't trust the world not to check his corners.

"We need to talk," I said, my voice more blunt than I meant it to be.

His eyes narrowed, instantly on guard. "What happened now?"

"Lucy," I said, pacing as I spoke. "She and Nick are going to his lake house next weekend. I think she might be Clay's next victim."

His jaw clenched, the name hitting him harder than I expected.

"Lucy Rivers? She's been around since they were kids. I never thought..." He trailed off, his weathered face folding into something grim. For a moment, he looked like he was about to punch a wall.

"If you're right, then I need to talk to him again."

"No." My voice came out too fast, too hard. I steadied it. "We can't risk that. If Clay surfaces, if Clay even sniffs confrontation, it's over. Too risky."

His silence was heavy, thick with something between shame and rage.

"I'll keep watch," I continued. "I'll watch Nick's house, Lucy, the lake house plans. I'll make sure nothing happens to her, or to Nick."

He looked at me, eyes dark with guilt. "Then take me with you. He's my son. If Clay's still out there... then this is on me too."

A bitter laugh escaped me before I could stop it.

"Never thought I'd be planning a stakeout with my best friend's dad."

"And what's wrong with that?" he said, trying to flex, his voice gruff. "Prison kept me sharp. Don't let the gray hair fool you." He flexed his knuckles, scarred and cracked, like he wanted to prove it.

I shook my head, a smirk tugging despite the tension. "Alright then. Let's get going."

We stocked up on gas station snacks and lukewarm coffee, the kind that coats your throat with grit.

Then we parked across from Nick's house, nights blending into one another under the cover of dark.

Sometimes Lucy stayed.

Sometimes she leaves.

Sometimes the windows stayed lit long past midnight.

Each night, I felt the same dread crawling closer, the fear that one of these nights, we wouldn't just be watching.

We'd be too late.

During the stakeouts, I always made a point to check in on Nick. It kept the routine alive, and it made the nights easier, for both of us.

"Everything good today?" I asked, leaning against the doorway like it was casual.

Nick looked tired, but he managed a faint smile.

"Yeah. Just writing. Trying not to overthink."

Nick rubbed his temple, like the words on the page were pressing too hard.

When he looked at me, it was just for a second, but something in his eyes felt colder than usual. Focused, calculating. Clay's stare, not Nick's. The smile that followed was tiring, almost forced, and I told myself I imagined it.

I nodded, forcing myself to stay calm even though I wanted to say a thousand things. "That's good. Keep at it. I'll be around later."

It wasn't much, but it was enough. If I broke the pattern, he'd notice and the last thing I needed was Nick, or worse Clay, questioning why I'm not around.

Walking away from his house, I hated the way it felt, like I was keeping him safe by lying to him. He thought I was checking in out of habit, maybe even friendship. But really, I was watching him like a case file.

I barely got any sleep. My mind kept circling back to the lake house. If Clay was planning something, it would be there.

It took hours of dead ends and cross-county records before the address finally appeared. I didn't stop to question it. I convinced Nick's dad to come with me.

***

A few days before Nick and Lucy's planned getaway, we drove out. The lake house sat half-hidden behind trees, too quiet, like it had been waiting for us. I'm not usually one to break the law, but slipping a lock like some cheap burglar felt less wrong than the thought of what might happen if I didn't.

We parked far away from the place, hidden off the road. It was a long walk through the trees, but I didn't want to risk my car being spotted anywhere near here.

If Clay had been by recently, or if he came back suddenly, I couldn't afford to leave a trail.

Nick's dad didn't say anything as we hiked up toward the house, but I could feel the weight of his silence. I glanced at his father. He looked older, smaller somehow, like the drive had already drained him.

I wondered if he knew, really knew, that tonight he wasn't just going to see a house. He was going to see the pieces of his son he'd been trying not to face.

Inside wasn't what I expected. Nick always liked modern, clean lines, light colors. This place felt heavy. Dark wood paneling, antique lamps, furniture that didn't belong to him. It was like Clay had decorated it himself or at least chosen it as his playground.

"Careful," I said, handing Nick's dad a pair of gloves. I tugged mine on. "Pick everything up and put it back exactly where you found it. We don't want Clay suspecting anyone's been here."

We split up. For a while, it was nothing but the sound of floorboards creaking beneath our weight. Dust, old books, bottles of scotch. Then, something caught my eye: a slight dip in the floor beneath the rug in the corner.

I pulled it back. Hollow. Weak. I pried up the loose boards and there it was, a box.

Inside were items I instantly recognized—journals and things I wished I didn't. Trinkets, jewelry, a folded scarf—souvenirs that carried the echo of the dead. My hands shook as I reached for them.

Nick's dad stepped up behind me, his shadow falling over the box. His face said everything, revulsion, grief, guilt, but he didn't speak. He couldn't.

I opened one of the journals.

Clay's handwriting was different from Nick's; meticulous, almost elegant, the kind that made the horror feel deliberate. Each page was a blueprint: dates, names, rituals, plans—details C. Holloway had omitted, some pages, a calculated smokescreen for anyone who looked too closely.

I read aloud, even as dread churned through me with every line:

She thought the water would save her, staring at the lake as if it held sanctuary. I held her under until the bubbles stopped—two minutes, thirty-four seconds. She gave up too fast. The scarf goes in the box... the rest of her stays with the fish.

My throat closed up. I forced myself to turn each page, even as my hands trembled, each entry worse than the one before, each word sinking like a stone in my gut.

Finally, I snapped photos of everything, flipping through as fast as I dared. We didn't have enough time. We needed to be gone before anyone returned—Clay, Nick... it didn't matter who.

I shut the journal and slid it back into the box, my hands shaking even under the gloves.

Nick's dad still hadn't said a word. His mouth set rigid, eyes glassy. I could feel the air between us thicken, and I couldn't tell if he was about to break down... or break something else entirely.

"We've got what we need," I muttered. "Let's get out of here."

***

As I turned toward the door to leave, headlights cut through the trees. Gravel crunched under tires, and my stomach dropped even further. Nick's car.

"Shit."

I froze, scanning the room for a way out. "Nick and Lucy are here already."

His dad didn't waste a second. "This way," he hissed, jerking his chin toward a narrow door at the back of the house.

We slipped through fast, feet thudding too loud on old wood floors, the chilly night air rushing against us as we pushed out the back. Why the hell were they early?

I ducked low, following his dad through the shadows, every twig crack sounding like a gunshot. I didn't see any security that would've set something off.

Nick's voice fainted through the walls as he spoke to Lucy, calm, casual. Like this was just a weekend getaway.

It wasn't.

Not anymore.

I crouched lower, night air heavy against my skin, goosebumps up my arms. Nick's dad and I stayed pressed against the side of the lake house, shadows swallowing us whole.

Through the thin wooden walls, voices bled through. Nick's voice—except it wasn't Nick. There was a detached, measured precision in his tone, each word wrapped in steel.

"You shouldn't question me, Lucy. You know what happens if you do."

I glanced at his dad. His lips pressed into a hard line, knuckles white as his hand clenched the house's side.

Lucy's reply floated through, softer, trembling. But there was a strange edge underneath it, like her fear was rehearsed.

"Nick, I just want to know why."

Nick's dad flinched, a curse under his breath. He thinks she's in danger. And for a second, I did too.

But something in her voice made my blood run cold. The way she stretched Nick's name. She knew it wasn't him.

Nick's voice dropped lower, coaxing, predatory.

"It has to. Tonight. You know why."

Silence followed, broken only by the creak of the floorboards as someone paced inside. My pulse hammered in my ears, drowning everything else.

Lucy's next words came like a knife sliding free of its sheath.

"Nick… what are you doing with that?"

What the hell were they talking about?

Nick's dad didn't hesitate. His whole body surged forward like instinct had snapped his leash.

"She's in trouble—"

"Wait!" I hissed, grabbing his arm. But he ripped free, shouldering through the back door like a battering ram. I had no choice but to follow.

The instant we stepped inside, the door behind us shut. Lucy was on the floor, her wide-eyed gasp was too perfect, like an actor hitting her mark.

"Adam! Mr. Smith! Please help!" hand pressed to her chest. Lamplight caught the glitter in her eyes—not fear, but expectation. Amateur acting, though—I saw right through it.

And Nick… or rather, Clay wearing Nick's skin… smiled. Not my friend's smile. This one was darker. Calculated.

"Lucy, that was beautiful." He said helping her up. Then he adjusts his posture as if expecting guests,

"Welcome to my house."

And just like that, the truth hit me.

We weren't saving anyone.

We were the ones caught.

Nick's dad looked dazed, confusion written across his face. I forced myself to stay calm or at least look calm.

Clay's grin stretched across his face, cold and sharp. "You thought you could outsmart me," he said, gesturing toward the floorboards. "See this?" He lifted a small device; a security trigger tucked beneath the wood. "The second your hand moved that box, I got a notification," he said, "good thing Nick decided to… step out for a little while."

I narrowed my eyes at Clay and Lucy, trying to find the words. "Lucy... you knew about everything?"

Before she could answer, Clay stepped closer, arm draped around her shoulders possessively.

"Lucy's been the most helpful," he said, almost chuckling. "Always supporting Nick."

I stared at her. "Why?"

"I just wanted to help," she said. "He needed me."

"And once we get rid of the two of you," Clay continued, circling us, "Nick can hide in the dark void forever."

I had to remind myself; this wasn't Nick. Not now.

Nick's dad squared his shoulders, stepping forward. "You don't get to use him, my son—for whatever game this is." His voice shook, but there was steel beneath it.

Clay tilted his head, smirk curling his lips.

"Game? No, no... this is protection, guidance. Something he needed, though he doesn't know it yet."

"You mean control," Nick's dad spat. "You're poisoning him, warping him!"

Clay's eyes softened, not warm, just unnervingly calm. "Twisting? Perhaps. But some things... some truths... he would never have survived otherwise."

Confusion and anger battled across Nick's dad's face. "What are you talking about?"

Clay leaned closer, voice low, like a whisper meant only for him. "Sometimes, to save someone, you must destroy the world around them first. He'll understand one day... maybe. But for now, he's under my protection."

Nick's dad's fists clenched. "Protection? You've gone too far."

Clay's smirk returned, "I protected him more than you have. Maybe I haven't gone far enough."

A pause stretched between them, heavy with unspoken threats. Clay's gaze flicked to me for just a second, calculating, before stepping back and letting the tension simmer, "Shall we see how far I can go?"

Clay lunged first. His punch connected with Nick's dad, and he crumpled to the floor, unconscious.

Rage and fear collided within me, a fire that made my hands shake. I couldn't let him hurt my friend—or anyone else.

I ducked and turned, keeping low as Clay circled me like a predator. Every creak of the floorboards.

My lungs were screaming for air. This isn't just a fight, I thought. This is a war over my best friend's life.

"Not fast enough!" I spat, shoving him away, narrowly avoiding a punch that would have shattered my jaw.

The lamp beside us toppled, glass shattering, sparks skittering across the floorboards. Shadows danced grotesquely across the walls, stretching his grin into something monstrous.

I could feel the weight of the journal in my mind—the twisted chronicles of his victims. Then Lucy's betrayal pressed at the edges of my thoughts, sharp as a blade. She'd been helping him... and now she stood somewhere just out of reach, enjoying the chaos.

For a brief second, I saw it—Nick. A flicker of hesitation in Clay's stride, a tremor in his voice. Hope stabbed through me. He's in there. Somewhere. I need to reach him.

Clay swung, and I blocked, rotating my body to avoid a direct hit. My knuckles grazed his chin as I pushed back, but his strength pinned me.

He laughed, a cruel, hollow sound.

"You really thought you could stop me?" he hissed, circling again. "Adam... reading the journal, sneaking into my house... you're already part of the story. And soon, you'll vanish like all the others."

I ducked, blood drumming in my veins, trying to calculate my next move. One wrong strike and Nick could be gone forever. I forced my hands to steady, muscles coiled tight as springs.

Then Clay struck.

Hard.

His fist connected with my cheek, pain exploding in stars across my vision.

The world tilted.

My knees buckled, and I staggered back, trying to stay upright.

I lunged, grabbing his arm, trying to pin him, trying to remember the Nick I knew.

"You're not him! You're not Nick!" I shouted, desperation clawing at my throat.

A flicker of something familiar—a softness in his eyes—made me hesitate.

And he exploited it. He twisted, elbow catching me in the side, wind knocked out of me. Pain radiated through my ribs. I stumbled, bracing myself on the floorboards.

Lucy moved suddenly, stepping between us. I reacted with instinct, shoving her aside. She hit the ground hard, letting out a muffled gasp. My stomach sank as I realized she was unconscious—but alive.

Clay surged forward, and we collided again, rolling across the floorboards, each of us grappling for control. My vision blurred with sweat and adrenaline.

Every second felt stretched, elastic. My muscles screamed, but I couldn't let him win—not now, not ever.

"I'm not giving up that easy," I growled, pinning him to the ground with every ounce of strength I could muster.

Clay's eyes flashed, a dark glint that was almost... familiar.

"Adam... what are you doing?"

His voice cut through the chaos, a taunting echo of Nick's tone.

For a fraction of a second, my heart leapt. Could it be him? Could it be Nick fighting back?

Then Clay's fist collided with my cheek, pain searing through my skull.

The world tipped sideways.

Stars exploded behind my eyes.

My grip loosened, the ground rushing up to meet me.

The last thing I saw before darkness swallowed me was the faintest flicker of something human in those eyes, a shadow of my friend struggling against the void.

And then... silence.

six

I blacked out again.

Usually, I wake up in my bed or slumped over my desk. But this time, when my vision cleared, I saw Adam lying unconscious right in front of me.

How did this happen?

I kneeled beside him, shaking my head. No... I didn't hurt him. I didn't hurt anyone.

But the lake house around me was chaos. Chairs overturned, glass shattered, the smell of sweat clinging to the air.

My head spun as my eyes swept the room. My dad, crumpled on the floor, groaned softly.

And Lucy... she was out cold, sprawled across the rug. A sick knot formed deep in me. I wasn't sure if I should feel anger, fear, or pity but the sight of her unconscious made me feel different.

Not for long, though.

I looked back over at Adam.

Nick. A voice slithered through the silence. *Look what you did to your best friend—your brother.*

"No!" My throat tore with the word. "You did this!"

The sound echoed, empty and useless.

I stumbled forward, pulse slamming against my skull, until I reached the mirror on the far wall. My reflection stares back, pale, shaking, wild-eyed.

"This wasn't me," I rasped.

Louder, I yelled, "I didn't hurt anyone!"

But then the glass froze.

My reflection stopped following me.

Clay stared back.

"Don't get sentimental, Nick," he says, his smile a razor's edge. "He was in the way."

"You hurt my friend." My voice cracked into a snarl. "That's where this ends."

Clay chuckled, low and venomous.

"You don't need him. You don't need anyone. You just need me."

"You're wrong!" I slammed my fist against the wall.

His eyes gleamed. Calm. Patient. Cruel.

"You can't even face your own past, Nick."

"Shut up!" I said, swinging my fist towards the mirror.

The mirror rippled like water, distorted. My reflection shrank, bones softening, until a younger version of me stares back. Twelve years old.

Tears streak his bruised face. His lips trembled as he whispered, "No... please don't hurt me."

My hand froze mid-swing, fist hovering just inches from the glass. The sight guts me. That was what I used to say, repeatedly, to survive.

"Please don't..." the boy whimpered again, until his expression curled into a grin.

The child's voice sharpened, mocking.

"Remember this one? The pathetic little kid, who hid under the bed while Dad raised his fist. The one who begged Mom to make him stop."

My chest caved in on itself. Shame burned hot, tangled with rage.

The boy tilted his head. Clay's voice poured from his mouth now, rich and cutting. "That's all you are, Nick. A scared little boy. I'm the one who survived. I'm the one who made you strong."

I dug my nails into my palms, trying to drown him out. But his words kept pressing, heavier, like the mirror itself is leaning closer, ready to swallow me whole.

"You didn't just hide, Nick," Clay sneered. "You let me take over. You wanted me to do the things you were too weak to do. Don't act like you don't know why I'm here."

"Shut up, shut up, shut up!"

My voice shreds in my throat as I slammed the words into the glass.

The reflection wavered, blurred, until it wasn't me anymore. It's her. My mother. Her eyes hollow, her lips trembled as she leaned toward me.

"Why did you do it, Nick?" she whispered.

"Why did you let me die?"

My throat tightened until I could barely breathe.

"No... no, that's not—"

Clay's voice curled from behind me like smoke, thick and suffocating.

"Didn't you?"

My twelve-year-old self stepped into view beside her in the mirror, shoulder to shoulder, smiling too wide.

"You wanted her gone."

"I didn't!"

My fists crashed into the mirror. The image shattered into a thousand ripples, but his voice echoed through the cracks.

Clay's reflection bled back into the broken glass, smirking through every shard.

"Sensitive topic, huh?"

I swallowed hard, the taste of iron on my tongue. "No."

The word comes out flat, dead. I felt numb, as if my body wasn't mine anymore.

"It won't be long before you break again," Clay murmured, his tone almost tender. "And when that happens, I'll be here. Because while everyone else leaves, I'll always stay."

"No." My voice shook, but I forced it steady.

"Not anymore. You don't control me," I said, even as the doubt clawed at me.

I tore my eyes from the glass and forced myself to breathe, my hands still stinging from the impact.

I pulled Adam off the floor and eased him onto the couch, my grip unsteady despite my efforts to keep it together. I looked at him then. Bruises are already darkening along his skin, proof of what I failed to stop.

He doesn't deserve this.

I grabbed a pen, scrawled out a note with trembling hands. He doesn't need to be dragged into my war. He's already done too much. If he gets hurt because of me, I'll never forgive myself.

Behind me, Clay's voice gnawed at the edges of my mind, low, mocking, insistent.

"That's right Nick, run away like you always do."

I tuned him out, focusing on Adam, on the words I leave behind.

This was the best choice. I need to disappear before Clay finds another way to use me. I need to face him alone.

Because if I don't… Adam will be next.

My dad groaned, a ragged sound that cuts through the quiet. "Nick…" he rasped, his face was taut with pain.

I ignored him, finishing the letter I'd left for Adam. My hands shook slightly as I folded it, then I gathered my few things, careful not to make a sound. Every movement felt heavier, like the air itself was pressing down on me.

"Nick… take me with you." His voice was rough, painful, but there's an urgency there that I couldn't entirely ignore.

I froze for a fraction of a second.

Why would I do that? After all these years? I'll never forgive him.

I clenched my teeth and kept moving, sliding my backpack over my shoulder.

"Nick… I know things you don't. Right now, you don't understand but give me a chance. Take me with you, please." His voice cracked, pleading, dragging at the edges of something I thought I buried long ago.

I stopped, turning slightly, my eyes hard. "If you have something to say, say it now. Don't waste my time."

He swallowed, pain flashing across his features.

"No… you don't know Clay like I do. If you want him gone, if you want this nightmare to end… take me with you. Let me help."

The room felt smaller, the shadows stretching longer across the floor. I wanted to walk away, but pressure builds in my chest; something between guilt, frustration, and fear.

I didn't even know he knew Clay existed.

I can hear the echo of Clay's voice from earlier, reminding me what's at stake.

If he knows who Clay is, maybe he can help. And right now, I need answers. Every instinct screamed to leave him behind. I motioned toward the door. "Come on, old man."

"Why does everyone keep calling me old?" he groaned, joints popped as he pushes himself up, but instead of following me, he scanned the room.

His voice comes rough, urgent. "Nick, wait, we can't leave Lucy like this. Help me find Adam's handcuffs."

The words froze me.

"What do you mean?"

He's already digging through the mess on the floor, hands trembling more from determination than age. When he finally pulled the cuffs free, the metal gleamed cold under the weak light.

"We can't trust her, Nick—" he started, clamping the cuffs around Lucy's wrists while she lied motionless.

"I can't trust you," I snapped, cutting him off.

That gets him.

He paused mid-motion, his eyes lifting to mine, heavy with something I couldn't read. Not anger. Not pride. Something closer to… regret.

For a second, he looked less like the man who failed me and more like a father trying to reach his son.

"We both can't trust Clay," he says finally, his voice steady, deliberate.

His gaze drifted to Lucy.

"And when Adam wakes up, he'll thank us for doing this. I'm glad you found a good friend to have around."

The words hung there, uneasy, as I glanced at Lucy's bound hands. I can't tell if he's being protective or paranoid. Maybe both.

The room felt narrower than before, the shadows clinging to the corners as if they didn't want to let us leave.

***

When we stepped outside, the night air smacked me across the face—cool, sharp, carrying the sting of truth I'm not ready for.

There's no going back now.

We reached my car. I slid behind the wheel, the cool leather against my back. The silence between us is thick, suffocating, heavier than the engine's low rumble.

I gripped the wheel too tight, knuckles aching, until finally I let the words spill.

"So… how do you know Clay?"

He hesitated, rubbing the back of his neck like he's pulling words out of some locked room. "I met him… when you were young."

I blinked, surprised. "You met him?" My voice comes out tense.

"Sounds unreal, right?" His tone was low, almost regretful. "I thought it was too." He left it there, heavy with unspoken warnings.

I gripped the wheel tighter. "Then what do you know about him?"

"He's not to be trusted." His eyes flicked to mine, serious, almost pleading. "I thought as you got older, he'd vanish. I thought he'd gone away. But... he's still here."

The words hung in the air like smoke.

"Still here... meaning?" I pressed, my pulse quickening.

"Meaning he's patient. Meaning he's clever. Meaning he's waiting for you to make the wrong move." His voice dropped, almost a whisper. "Meaning he knows exactly how to use what he sees in you... against you. He's probably paying attention to this conversation right now."

I stared at the dark road, headlights slicing through the trees. "What do you mean, use me against me?"

He swallowed hard.

"When you were a kid... he knew your fears, your shame. He knew how far you'd go to survive. And he's been shaping you, Nick... like a shadow. Every time you think you're alone, every time you think you're making your own choice, he's been there. Guiding, waiting."

Dread twisted inside me.

"So… Lucy? Adam? All of this?"

His gaze dropped, shadowed.

"All of it. He doesn't play fair. He doesn't care who's in his way. Not you, not anyone. And Lucy… I thought she'd be gone by now."

"Gone?" My voice cracked. "What are you talking about?"

My dad studied me. "How much do you remember from your childhood?"

I sat there, silent, because the truth is I don't trust my own memories. Not anymore. He gave me a look, the kind that said he already knew the answer.

I could barely breathe. I forced my voice out, trying to steer the conversation somewhere—anywhere—I could handle. "So, what, you're telling me you've dealt with Clay before?"

His nod was slow, deliberate. "More than you know. I tried to stop him… failed. I thought taking you to church when you were a kid would be enough. I was wrong."

The car felt smaller now, the air heavy with his confession.

"Except Mom was the one who took me to church."

Silence stretched between us, thick, suffocating. He stared out the windshield before finally speaking, voice low, almost breaking.

"You're right… she did take you, son."

He was lying. And I knew why.

I glanced at him, eyes narrowing. The street-lights flickered across his face, casting long shadows in the car. There's something he's not telling me, something buried beneath his words, and I can feel it like a pulse in the quiet.

I could hear his breath, measured, cautious. "I made mistakes, Nick. Big ones. But I never wanted to hurt you," he said finally.

I kept my eyes on the road, letting the tension build with every mile. The streetlights flickered again, quick and fleeting, like reminders of every moment I'd been left exposed.

"You didn't stop him," I said finally, voice low.

"You left gaps. You left me. You created him."

"I know," he admitted quietly, almost a whisper, "I didn't protect you enough. I thought I could shield you, but Clay… he's clever. He's always been clever. I should have done more."

A knot of anger formed within me, but fear and something like guilt kept my hands steady on the wheel. I wanted to shout, to throw every word back at him, but I stayed silent.

"So, what, you think you can help me now?" I asked, glancing at him briefly from the corner of my eye. His expression was hard to read, but I could see the weight pressing down behind it.

"I don't know," he admitted. "But I'm not leaving you alone in this. Not again."

The car fell silent, nothing but the hum of the tires. But even in that quiet, I could feel Clay's voice pressing in the back of my mind, a whisper reminding me that nothing was safe, not even the truth.

I wasn't sure what to believe. I've gone almost half of my life hating my dad. I told myself I wouldn't forgive him, not for killing mom.

How could I?

Something in me wanted to believe him.

If someone were to get hurt helping me, I'd rather have it be him, than Adam.

But as soon as the thought settled, I froze.

Was that me? Or was that, Clay?

The words echoed too harsh, too cruel, like a splinter lodged under my skin. I told myself I was only being protective of Adam, but the truth was uglier than that. It felt like Clay whispering through me, turning loyalty into something venomous.

Maybe that's what he wanted—to make me doubt myself until I couldn't tell where I ended and he began.

I gripped the wheel tighter, the hum of the tires filling the silence. I wasn't sure where I was driving, only that I needed somewhere quiet, safe. Somewhere I could breathe without feeling him watching me from the inside out.

I couldn't stop replaying the thought in my head. Did I really want to see my dad get hurt? Or was that Clay planting the idea, just to make me flinch?

The more I questioned it, the less I trusted myself. My own mind felt like a crime scene. Every thought, every memory smeared with fingerprints that weren't mine.

Without thinking, I drove to my mom's grave. My dad's reaction would say it all. Pulling into the graveyard, I caught his eyes—alert, wary, like he already knew why we were here.

"Is this where she's—?"

His voice broke off mid-sentence. He went pale, lips pressed firm, like he might throw up.

I parked without a word, and together we stepped out. I led him down the narrow path, each step crunching over frost-tipped grass, until we reached her headstone.

For a long moment, nothing.

Then my dad dropped to his knees, shoulders shaking. "I'm sorry… I'm so, so sorry."

I watched him closely. Was this real? Or just the practiced remorse of a man who'd spent years behind bars? Or maybe… time had finally worn him down, leaving only regret.

I stayed back, letting him grieve, though a part of me wanted to step in, to tell him it wasn't real, that he didn't deserve forgiveness.

But another voice familiar, low, pressing, nudged me.

Watch him. See how he reacts. Does he really feel this? Or is this what he wants you to see?

I shook my head slightly, trying to push it away. Clay.

Always Clay, always weaving the edges of my thoughts until I couldn't tell what was mine.

"You didn't deserve this. You deserved better. I wanted you to get help…" His fist slammed into the ground beside the grave, a burst of anger breaking through.

Then, almost at once, he took a deep, shuddering breath. "I wanted you to be happy," he said, tears streaming down his face.

Why did it seem like he cared about Mom? Unease coiled my stomach. A sudden flashback hit me, replacing the memory I had of him murdering her: him crying over her corpse, raw and broken, while I watched from around the corner.

I looked down at my hands.

Did I do this?

Was it all Clay's whispering, twisting my thoughts until I couldn't trust a single one?

Did he want me to think my dad never cared?

But look at what he did and how he's reacting now.

Clay, always creeping, always probing.

My dad's eyes met mine, knowing and steady, as if he could see the void I was spiraling into. Without hesitation, he reached for my hand. "Come on. We need to go somewhere."

The sun was climbing, spilling pale light over the gravestones. I didn't resist. I followed him, every step heavy, the morning air smelling faintly of damp earth and new beginnings.

Where was he taking me? I didn't know, but a part of me hoped it was somewhere safe—somewhere I could breathe, even if only for a little while.

I hadn't gotten much sleep, and the weight of everything pressing down on me made my eyelids heavy. I drifted off in the car as my dad drove, the hum of the engine a dull lullaby. Flashbacks surged into my dreams, tangling and overlapping—what I thought was real, what could have been, and what Clay might be whispering in the shadows of my mind.

***

First, it's my childhood kitchen. Sunlight pools across the floor, Mom laughing, stirring the pot, warm and soft. I reach for her, and the walls ripple like liquid, the floor bending under my feet, stretching, folding in on itself.

The laughter bends, loops, elongates, and then, snap, the light fractures.

Now the air is thick, metallic, tasting faintly of rust and old smoke.

The laughter isn't Mom's anymore, it's him. My dad, smiling, but the smile slips, melting, dripping down his face like candle wax.

Mom's voice flickers around me, overlapping, looping, zigzagging between the gentle words I thought I remembered and the jagged reality of her drunken screams.

Clay whispers, low.

Look closer… decide what's real… don't blink…

The ceiling liquefies, dripping down in strands of color, pooling at my feet. I stumble backward, hands gripping walls that shiver and breathe, doors melting into mirrors, mirrors melting into doors.

My dad's face stretches, distorts, contorting into Mom's, then back again, their features sliding into each other like different-colored paint mixing in together.

Suddenly I'm in my bedroom. The walls stretch taller, then collapse sideways, raining fragments of memories, shards of laughter, shouting, slamming doors, whispered threats.

"This is all your fault…"

Dad's voice splits, splits again, some of its mom's.

My small hands slam against walls that breathe and pulse, reaching for something to hold, but it dissolves beneath my touch.

I run, and the hallway stretches into infinity, the floor rippling like water. The light bends, folding over itself in impossible angles. Rooms open and close like lungs, each one has a fractured memory. Sometimes Mom, sometimes Dad—but all their faces and voices are bleeding into each other.

Clay's voice coils around my skull, playful and menacing.

Decide. What's yours? What's mine? Look closer. Don't turn away.

My body feels fluid and weightless. The floor is gone, replaced by a swirling kaleidoscope of memories and half-truths.

Hands that look like mine stretch across the air, grasping at shadows, grasping at melted fragments of reality. I gasp, trying to scream, but my voice distorts, loops, bouncing back at me like broken glass. Shapes bloom and collapse—my mother's anger, my father's laughter, then my mother's laughter and my father's anger.

Finally, my own face staring back, melting into a grin that isn't mine. The colors swirl as the walls pulse. Every step, every thought, is smeared, doubled, split—like I'm falling through a hall of mirrors made of liquid memory.

Clay's whispers follow, a steady, hypnotic drip: *Don't flinch. Don't forget. Decide.*

A solid edge—fingers closing around mine. My dad's hand? Or my own? I can't tell, only that it anchors me, dragging me out of the dissolving nightmare.

***

The dream fractured like glass, and I jolted awake in the passenger seat, heart pounding.

"You alright?" Dad's voice cuts through the fog, steady but edged with concern. His eyes flicked to me, softer than I expected. "Looked like you were having a nightmare."

I rubbed my face, forcing my voice even. "I'm fine." A lie. My gaze drifted out the window, and that's when I saw it—the looming steeple, the wooden cross catching pale morning light. My stomach knotted.

"We're here," he says simply.

I felt panic setting in. "Why… this place?"

He didn't answer. Just opened the door, the creak of the hinges broke the silence, and started walking towards the entrance with quiet determination.

Something in me wanted to stay in the car, but my legs betrayed me. I followed.

***

Inside, the air is cool, heavy with candle wax and old wood polish. Dusty light filters through stained glass, splashing fractured colors across the pews.

My dad slid into one near the front and bowed his head. His lips moved soundlessly, and for a moment he looked like a man I didn't know—small, humbled, almost broken.

I sat beside him, restless, my eyes scanning the arches, the altar, the crucifix.

Memories press in like ghosts. My mother's hand tugging mine down this very aisle. The priest's booming voice I thought I'd forgotten. I don't know if the images are real or another trick of Clay's, but they wouldn't leave me.

A figure stepped into the aisle; one I recognized from confession.

The priests eyes caught mine immediately, recognition lighting them. "It's you." he said, surprise and warmth threading his voice.

A chill ran through me. I remembered what I'd told him—the blackouts, the things I couldn't control. He didn't flinch or recoil; just nodded, quietly, as if he had carried it with him all this time. That silent acknowledgment made my chest tighten.

Before I could respond, my dad rose, a small, weathered smile softening his face. "Father Bob. It's been too long." He embraced him briefly, and I caught a glimpse of the man he used to be.

"Welcome back," the priest says warmly. "I never thought I'd see you here again, especially with…" His gaze lingered on me, searching.

"My son," Dad says without hesitation, pride threading through his voice. "This is Nick. Grown now, but still my boy."

Father Bob's expression softened further.

"Nick... you were here not too long ago, I didn't know this was your dad. I remember you, that boy from years ago, coming to church with him."

I laughed, but it came out hollow.

"That's strange. I don't remember it that way."

The priest's eyes flicked to me, then back to my father.

A pause.

Something unspoken passed between them.

My dad held his gaze, steady, as if they've had this conversation before, without me.

"What?" I demand. "What are you not saying?"

Neither of them answered.

Clay slithered into my mind.

You see that? They're scared.

"Shut up." I blurted, my voice betraying me, though I was talking to him.

My dad had concern etched across his face, but he stayed silent. Father Bob opens his mouth, about to speak, but my dad gently raises a hand, stopping him.

"I don't know what to believe," I say, voice calm at first, then rising, echoing against the stone walls.

"I can't tell what's real anymore!"

My hands are clenched, the pew rattling under my grip. Silence swallowed the church.

Even Clay is quiet. Like he knew I just exposed myself exactly how he wanted—helpless, rattled, unsure.

I looked at Father Bob, then my dad, as my pulse spiked.

"I'm not crazy."

"No one said you were crazy, Nick," my dad said calmly.

My voice started steady, but somewhere in between, it hardens, tenses up, like Clay has his hands on my throat, forcing the words out.

"You don't have to say anything—I can see it on your faces. The way you're judging me."

Father Bob opens his mouth, gentle, but I slice through it.

"You think I'm dangerous, don't you? You don't even know if it's me standing here... or him."

"Nick," my dad says, steady but quiet, hands open like he's approaching a wounded animal.

"Nobody thinks you're dangerous."

I laughed. Too sharp. Too bitter. It rattled off the stone walls, ugly and alien, even to my own ears.

"Not dangerous? Then why does he keep coming back? Why do I see him every time I close my eyes? Why do I keep blacking out?"

My voice broke, then spiked again, ragged.

"He's here, Dad! He exists—and he's me."

The silence that followed was suffocating.

Father Bob's face drained of color, lips pressed firm like he's praying for the right words but can't find them. My dad just looked older, hollowed out, but his eyes burned with something I couldn't name—guilt, pity... or fear.

Clay leaned in, velvet and venom:

There it is. Now they know. You can't hide me anymore.

"I'm not crazy," I whispered, but it didn't sound convincing, not even to me.

My dad took a step closer.

"Son, listen to me—"

"Don't call me that!" The words ripped out of me, too loud, too raw. For a split second, it didn't even sound like my voice at all.

The church froze, the air thick and unmoving, even the walls were holding their breath.

The creak of the doors drew my attention—parishioners shuffled in for morning mass. Their whispers echoed like accusations, every glance cutting into me. Heat crawled up the back of my neck. I couldn't breathe.

I glared at my dad.

"You know what? I don't need your help. Forget this."

"Nick—"

He reached for me, but I tore myself away, my voice cracked harsh enough to sting.

"I don't need help!"

My pulse was racing, panic blooming fast and suffocating. Clay's thoughts bled into mine, twisting, binding, until I can't tell where he ends and I begin.

Leaving is the only way. The only chance to protect him. To protect anyone.

I stumbled into the sunlight; the church bells rang overhead like mockery.

My hands shook as I fumbled the keys, but I finally slammed the car door shut. The engine roared to life, vibrating through me. I turned off my phone, I didn't think about where I was going, just that I needed to leave. Nowhere, anywhere, as long as it's away.

***

By noon, I reached Crescent Lakes, the RV I'd stashed waiting quietly at the secluded campground. A quick check, supplies loaded, and I'm on the road again.

Hours passed, as the sun arced high then dipped low, painting the sky in bruised purples and fiery reds. The tires hum on asphalt, the landscape shifting mile by mile.

By evening, I pulled into a remote campsite far from the nearest road, gravel crunching beneath the wheels. Tall pines stood sentinel on either side, shadows lengthening. The air is thick with quiet, the kind that listens, and for the first time all day, I let it settle around me.

Inside, I locked the door, the latch clicking with finality.

The world outside—Adam, Lucy, my dad—shrank to nothing. The hum of the RV's small fridge, the faint creak of its frame settling, becomes my only companion.

But Clay didn't care about walls or doors. He's there the instant I let my guard down. His voice slithered through my thoughts: *Nice little hideaway. You think you're safe here? You think you can run from me?*

I clenched the edge of the counter, my knuckles whitened.

"Quiet!" I snapped, but even as the words left my mouth, I know it's futile. He's not just in my head, he's me, or he's becoming me.

I threw myself onto the small couch, pulling a blanket over my legs, trying to breathe past the panic.

There's no phone, no distractions, no one to reach out to. Just me, the RV, and Clay whispering behind my eyes.

Outside, the wind rustles the trees, leaves scratching at the roof like fingernails. I closed my eyes and tried to sleep. But I knew it was a trap. Clay will feed on my solitude. And soon, he'll test me, push me to the edge.

Because no matter how far I drive, no matter how secluded I get... I can't escape him.

***

I rose unsteadily to pace, tripping over the edge of the small couch. My shadow stretched along the walls, distorted, monstrous.

And then I saw him—my own reflection in the tiny window.

Not me.

Clay.

Smiling, leaning close, whispering again.

You wanted to escape. But you can't. Not from me. Not from yourself.

I collapsed back onto the couch, panting. I closed my eyes, trying to summon any fragment of my own mind.

This is just me.

I'm in control.

I can fight him.

But Clay laughed, low and silk-like.

Control? That's funny. That's cute. Let's see how long you last, Nick.

***

I woke up to the shrill chirping of birds, scratching at the edges of my half-remembered dreams.

For a moment, I forgot where I was, the RV was quiet except for the occasional creak as it settled. The morning sunlight filtered through the blinds in harsh lines, cutting across the floor like accusations.

My body ached from the drive, every muscle tight from hours of holding the wheel. But worse than physical exhaustion was the weight, the knot of anxiety that wouldn't loosen.

Did Adam find my note?

Was Lucy okay?

My mind jumped ahead, filled with questions, accusations, judgment.

I grabbed a simple breakfast from the tiny kitchen in my RV—granola bar, lukewarm coffee, nothing fancy.

I sat at the small table, notebook open, pen poised but hovering.

What should I write?

Something publishable, maybe—a story someone could read without knowing the truth. Or maybe
a letter, a final goodbye for those who'd notice if I
vanished. Maybe a little of both.

I scribbled the first line, then tore it out, crum-
pling it in my hand before tossing it aside.

Nothing felt right.

Words felt like a lie or a confession I wasn't
ready to make. Still, I kept trying, letting the pen
scratch over paper, tracing my thoughts, my fear, my
plans in a haze of ink and coffee-stained pages.

Maybe this will be the story of someone who ran
too far. Or maybe just a way to remember myself in
case no one else ever will.

I put pen to paper; the nib scratched softly
against the page. Words came slow at first, hesitant,
like evaluating the ground before stepping.

*The road unwinds before him, a thin thread
through a world too vast, and he moves along it, hoping the miles will wash him away.*

I paused, staring out the RV window, watching
the trees, and felt the weight of my own sins pressing
down against my chest.

*His sins lie in him like stones in a pocket, heavy
and jagged. Every step shakes them loose; every mile*

turns them over, showing him edges he cannot smooth.

My hand trembled slightly as I wrote, the motion was both a release and a reminder of how much I've carried alone.

He is alone, but not free, wandering through a landscape that mirrors the deserts inside him.

I sipped my coffee, bitter, grounding me in the present, but the emptiness of the road stretched on in my mind.

Maybe someone will read this someday, and maybe they'll understand. Or maybe it's just a map of where I fell, so no one else follows the same path.

Setting the pen down for a moment, I stared at the words. Writing it made the silence less suffocating, even if only for a while.

I slammed the notebook shut, shoving it onto the passenger seat.

Clay's voice curled on the edges of my mind, soft but strong, whispering doubts and reminders of every mistake I've tried to bury.

You can't escape. You never could.

I started the engine, the rumble grounding me as I pulled onto the highway.

The first stop was gas. The pump hissed, and the smell of fuel filled my nose. I glanced around the empty lot, the sun climbing higher, reflecting off the metal of the RV.

I stocked up on snacks and grabbed a case of bottled water from the convenience store, eating in the cab while checking the map. The act of eating felt ordinary, almost comforting—a small tether to reality in the chaos of my thoughts, though Clay's voice was never far, whispering that I'm wasting time.

Clay's whispers were there between bites.

You think you can leave it all behind?

You know what's coming.

I threw the wrapper into the trash, shaking my head.

No. Not now.

Not while I'm moving.

The sun was lower now; the shadows stretched across the road. Clay's voice grew louder, more insistent, but I pressed the accelerator, focusing on the horizon, the bends of the road, the hum of the tires on asphalt. Every mile I put between me and Crescent Lakes is a small victory, a reminder that at least for now, I have control.

Evening settled around me, the sky painted in fiery reds. I pulled off the highway, stopping at a small rest area to stretch and take in the views.

Clay was quiet for a moment, but I knew it wouldn't last.

The road was empty and the quiet stretched on, broken only by the hum of the RV and the occasional whisper of wind against the windows. I tried to think of something, anything else.

By the time I pulled into a small, secluded clearing near Angel Point, night had fully fallen. The gravel crunched under the tires as I parked in an isolated lot that leaned like silent sentinels over the edge of the canyon.

I stepped outside, stretching, breathing in the cold, crisp desert air. Silence pressed in, heavy but not empty. I could feel him listening, waiting. Clay was still there, whispering from the shadows, but I've made it this far. I've survived the day, and for now, that's enough.

***

Suddenly, a camper emerged from the large brushes, stepping onto the gravel like he grew out of it. "Oh, sorry, man! Didn't even see you there," he says, brushing imaginary dust from his sweatshirt.

"All good," I replied, trying not to roll my eyes.

He looked like a walking stereotype of a hiking-hippie, bandana, messy hair, beaded necklaces, and a faint smell of patchouli that made me want to cough. He already looked baked beyond recognition.

"So... uh... what brings you out here?" he asked, swaying slightly as he talked.

"Just traveling," I said cautiously.

"Wanna try some edibles?" He held out a small, crumpled bag.

I raised an eyebrow.

Stranger danger is one thing, but I'm already teetering on the edge of my own low point. Maybe a chocolate or two wouldn't hurt.

"They're good," he says, holding out the little bag. "Really good. Come on... it's just a chocolate. You'll see." He grinned; fist extended like some handshake deal.

Something in his smile was infectious. Laid-back, harmless, or at least he seems harmless. I found myself hesitating for just a beat before the weird little voice in my head muttered, *why not?*

"Why me?" I asked as I completed his fist bump.

"Dude... we were brought together. Right here, right now. Plus, you look tense as a coiled spring. I think you need it man." he said, squinting at me like he's delivering life advice.

Too serious to be sober, too chill to be threatening.

Without overthinking it, I popped two in my mouth.

Worst case scenario?

I'm already chasing rock bottom.

"Oh—uh. I'm Brian, by the way." he said, like it just occurred to him. He rubbed the back of his neck, smiling easily. "Probably should've led with that."

"Nick," I say.

Brian nodded, like that's all he needed. He dropped down onto a boulder across from me, elbows on his knees.

"So, what brings you out here, Nick?"

I shrugged, "Driving. Thinking. Needed to get out of my head."

"Yeah," he says, like he gets it. "Same, honestly. Works been a drag. Just traveling. Figured I should see the world while I still can."

"Traveling alone?"

Brian shook his head, grinning. "Nah… she's asleep in the car with the dogs. Figured I'd stretch my legs."

I nodded, more understanding in that moment than I expected.

"So… uh… how long until this weed kicks in?" I asked, trying to sound casual.

He laughed; a high, airy sound that made the cacti seem like they were swaying in rhythm.

"Weed? Nah, man. These are shrooms."

He continued laughing as if he couldn't control it.

I blinked.

Then blink again.

Somehow, I'm both terrified and oddly amused.

"I do got some bud, though. Helps relax you for the trip," he said, pulling out a pack of rolling papers and expertly rolling a joint like it's second nature.

"Shrooms should take over in about an hour."

I watched, dumbfounded. The way his fingers moved, the concentration on his face... I can't believe this is happening. My heart raced a little, half in shock, half in weird anticipation.

"I'm guessing this is your first time with shrooms?" he asked, chuckling, not really because it's funny, but because, well... he's clearly in his own altered state.

He lit the joint and took a puff, immediately coughing like he's inhaling a volcano. Then he handed it to me.

I took a hit. Coughing erupted before I could think, harsh and uncontrollable. It's been years since I've smoked. Clay wouldn't approve anyway. My eyes water, and I hacked again, but somewhere beneath the discomfort, there's a flicker of… curiosity.

I followed him over to a weathered picnic table tucked beneath a cluster of brushes, cacti and boulders. We sat, legs dangling over the edge, the chocolates still lingering at the back of my mind. Above us, the first stars pricked the sky, tiny flickers against the deepening navy. The air smelled of shrubs, dust, and something wild, something free.

"So… your wife lets you do shrooms?" I asked, curiosity cutting through the haze.

Brian laughed softly, leaning back, hands behind his head. "Yeah, actually. Not sure how I got lucky enough to call her my wife. She drove today, so I'm letting her sleep."

I nodded, a little surprised.

"Huh. That's… chill."

"Chill's the word," he says, grinning. "But hey, also… don't overthink it. Just let it hit you."

"Don't overthink." I said laughing.

"This is the best place to watch the stars," he said, leaning back, eyes half-closed. "Ever just lie down and let the wind tell you stuff?"

I tilted my head, staring upward, letting the vastness swallow me. "Listen to the wind, huh?" I muttered. I felt lighter, the tight coil of thoughts loosening.

He nudged me with his shoulder. "The universe doesn't lie, man. It just… shows you what's already there. You see it or you don't."

I let my mind drift, watching the constellations blur and shift. Beneath the glittering black, thoughts crept in, every choice I've made lately, every knot I couldn't untangle. It's strange, but under these stars, it felt like a whisper, a faint pattern forming, hints of influence threading through my life.

"Ever feel like someone's been… arranging your life?" I murmured, almost to myself.

Brian chuckled, smoke curling lazily from the joint between his fingers.

"Maybe. Maybe it's God, the universe, maybe some other energy. Doesn't matter. What matters is you notice. Now… what are you going to do about it?"

I inhaled the fresh night air, letting it mingle with the smoke. For the first time in ages, I didn't fight the thoughts. I let them flow, watching the patterns, glimpses of truths I'm not ready to fully name.

A strange lightness settled over me, like I've lifted slightly above my own head. Not freedom yet, but enough to breathe, to see, to start untangling the path ahead.

"I don't think there's anything I can do about it," I murmured, soft and almost amused, letting the words dissolve into the night.

And yet, beneath the night sky, the world bloomed. The sky stretched and curved, folding over itself like wet fabric. Colors pulsed and rippled—cobalt and violet merging, then tearing apart into sparks of silver that spin lazily, like galaxies on a carousel.

The shrubs breathe with me, inhaling shadows and exhaling light. Every sound is liquid, every whisper of wind a note in a symphony I can't name.

My chest lifts and falls with the rhythm of something larger than mine. Patterns swam around me, constellations threading and unraveling before my eyes. I saw faces in the bark, smiles in the stones, and laughter in the ripple of a distant river.

Time bends, stretches, and folds, and I feel it all—the past, the now, the what's-to-come—not as pressure, but as texture beneath my skin.

Somewhere in the swirl, a quiet knowing settled. Not clarity about the how or why, not judgment, not even fear.

Just recognition.

Truths exist in the folds of the world whether I touch them or not. I breathe, and with each inhale, the weight loosens. Colors bled into one another, and yet every hue felt precise, intentional, like the universe was painting exactly what it needed me to see.

I imagined folding the threads of my life into something manageable, something I can carry without breaking. The truth, whatever shape it took—wasn't mine to fight right now. But it doesn't need to crush me either.

For the first time in ages, I felt light. I can let it sit, let it exist, and keep walking forward. Still keep laughing. Still keep seeing the patterns, the possibilities, the stars above.

I pressed my palm over my heart, trying to hold onto the warmth, the ease, the quiet certainty. I whispered to myself, softly, almost a promise: stay here, just a little longer. The colors shimmered, the cacti swayed, the stars hummed their silver songs—and for one perfect moment, I am here, fully, and I don't want to let go.

"Beautiful, isn't it?" Brian says, watching my reaction, as if he knew exactly how I felt.

Hours went by, and I'm not sure when he left, but I drifted off under the moon.

**

I woke up to the pale morning light hitting directly in my eyes while the birds sang, the RV nestled in the open campgrounds like a toy in a diorama.

My body felt heavy and humming, still vibrating with last night's clarity. I stepped onto the dry desert floor, the scent of shrubs and dry earth filled my lungs as I took a deep, steady breath.

Something dark caught my eye—streaks across the dirt, leading toward the river.

Blood?

Dark red stains on the desert ground, trailing toward the river that glints like liquid silver in the sun.

My heart stumbled.

The blood seemed impossibly out of place, a violent slash against the calm of desert.

Where did it come from? How did it get here?

My mind races.

Did something happen last night? Did I do this? Did Clay…?

It was quiet, the sunlight too bright, the shadows too deep. Every instinct screamed at me to run, to check, to fix—but I couldn't even move. Anxiety hammered through me, like it was trying to squeeze out the panic before I even knew what it was about.

I clutched at the warmth I felt last night, at the clarity I thought I'd found, but it slipped through my fingers, leaving only the pulse of fear and the echo of my own overreaction.

And then it hit me—all the memories. Every single one I'd buried, I remembered them all last night, and it broke me all over again.

Clay's voice crept in.

You think you can stop this?

I froze. It's like he's hearing my thoughts right out of my skull. During the shroom trip, I saw it, his side of the story, the memories I forced onto him, every move he made when he shoved me aside. And for some reason, I'm not afraid of him anymore.

All I could think about was Adam—and how he might already be in danger.

Unfortunately, I'd left without my phone, which meant I couldn't be traced. I darted to the RV and sped toward the nearest gas station, desperate for a way to reach him. Leaving the red stains behind.

Clay's voice slithered through my head again.

You're too late.

I shoved the thought down. I couldn't let him win.

***

Pulling into the gas station, I spotted a pay phone bolted outside the building. But before I could make it over, the door swung open and out walked a familiar figure—Brian. His arm is bandaged now. Relief washed over me.

He was alive.

I almost called out, wanted to thank him for the night, but I couldn't waste another second. I tugged my hood low, turned my back, and headed straight for the phone.

The cold metal swallowed my coins as I dialed Adam's number.

Straight to voicemail.

I tried again.

Nothing.

One more time—same.

Finally, I left a message, voice low and rushed.

"Adam... listen. I don't have time. You're in danger, okay? Don't trust her. Please, just—don't. I'll explain when I see you. God, I better see you. If you get this in time... I'll see you in Death Valley."

The desert stretched endlessly, pale gold under the rising sun. My hands gripped the wheel tighter than they needed to, knuckles white. Trying to process everything from last night, every memory I'd buried, every truth I'd forced myself to forget was back.

Lucy was out there, somewhere. And Adam... he didn't know.

Not yet.

I flicked the rearview mirror, scanning the road behind me. My mind raced faster than the RV's tires could spin. I couldn't afford mistakes, not now. Not when everything I'd remembered could save me... or destroy me.

Clay slipped into my mind here and there, like a shadow brushing against the edges of my thoughts. He didn't bother me the way he used to. If anything, it felt like he was trying to protect me, but I don't need him anymore.

You think you can do this without me? His voice hisses, just at the edge of my consciousness.

I gritted my teeth, almost smiling. I could feel his frustration, quiet and simmering, as if he hated that I've learned to stand on my own.

Clay slithered into my thoughts again, sharper this time, like ice in my veins. *You're walking straight into her trap.* He growled. *You can't protect Adam alone. You'll fail just like last time.*

I clenched the wheel, letting the tires hum against the asphalt. "I don't need you, Clay. I'm not afraid anymore," I bit back, feeling my pulse spiking.

Not afraid? You're blind! His voice cracked through my mind, anger and panic mingling. *She's not just a girl, Nick. She's clever, she's dangerous. One mistake and it's over.*

I swallowed hard, my knuckles white on the wheel.

"I'll take that risk. I have to."

A silence stretched between us, thick and suffocating, but I could feel him seething, simmering, trapped at the edges of my consciousness. I didn't need him.

Not this time.

"Why did you help her, Clay?" I hissed; eyes fixed on the endless strip of highway. The words slipped out before I could stop them.

A low chuckle echoes in my head.

Help her? I saved you. I gave her what she wanted so she'd leave you alive. She was using you.

"You knew," I snapped, heat burning up my chest. "All those nights I blacked out, you knew it wasn't me. You let her use us."

His voice was intense, furious now.

You wouldn't survive without me. You're too weak. She needed me. You needed me.

"No," I whisper, shaking my head. "You needed her."

The silence after Clay fades lingered in my head.

I stopped at another gas station on the edge of nowhere, stocking up on more water and food. Just enough to keep me going a while longer. After this, there's only Death Valley.

The hours blurred together as the desert swallows the road. My thoughts gnawed at me, Adam. Was he all right? Did Lucy get to him too? And Lucy… how could she twist everything, dragging me this far down with her?

seven

Waking up felt like being punched in the gut—maybe because I had been.

Slowly, I drifted back toward consciousness and heard someone moving nearby. My mind raced, trying to piece together what had happened.

Who could be here?

I kept my eyes shut, pretending to sleep. And then it clicked.

Lucy.

What was she doing? What was she planning?

"Shit. How did I end up here?" she muttered under her breath. "What happened?"

The faint clink of metal told me her cuffs were moving as she did. Then I heard a crinkle, the soft unfolding of paper.

"A note from Nick?" she whispered, voice uncertain as she tucked the paper away, almost like she was figuring things out herself.

Her movements grew closer. My pulse jumped. I cracked one eye open. She was right above me, leaning in.

Calmly, I slipped my hand into my pocket, felt the cool metal of the keys, and pulled them out. I dangled them just out of her reach, smirking. "Looking for these?"

Her eyes widened, innocence flooding her face.

"Adam, what the hell? How did I even get here? Where are we?" Her voice cracked, trembling, like she was terrified.

"Don't bullshit me, Lucy. I can see right through you." I kept my eyes locked on hers, refusing to fall for the act.

But she doubled down.

"Adam, this isn't funny. Why would you do this? I… I woke up in handcuffs. I don't even remember how I got here." Her voice shook, every word dripping with confusion, maybe fear.

Classic case of fake amnesia.

I narrowed my eyes, slipping the keys back into my pocket. "You don't remember, huh? That's convenient."

Her lips parted, trembling just enough to look real. "Adam, please. I don't know why I'm here."

"Well," I said slowly, tilting my head, "I wonder why you're the one in handcuffs, then."

Color drained from her face, but she didn't break.

"I don't know! I swear, I woke up like this. Someone… someone must've done this to me." Her voice rose, echoing through the quiet lake house as she looked at me as if she figured it out. "You. What do you want with me?"

I pinched the bridge of my nose, exhaling slowly. She was good. Real good. If I didn't know better, maybe I'd even believe her.

I dropped my hand and leveled my eyes at her.

"You're really going to play that card? Come on, Lucy. If I wanted something from you, do you think we'd be sitting here having this little chat?"

Her lips trembled, her whole body trembling like prey cornered.

"Then why am I here?" she whispered.

Her hands trembled against her scalp, the cuffs clinking with every movement. "You don't get it, Adam. My head is killing me. I don't even remember last night. What if you did this? What if Nick was right about you?"

That one landed sharper than the rest. She said it quick, almost too quick, like it had been waiting on her tongue.

I narrowed my eyes. "Nick was right about me? That's the best you've got?"

I leaned back in the chair, letting the silence stretch between us.

"Funny thing, Lucy, if I really did all the things you're trying to pin on me, you wouldn't be sitting here breathing."

Her face faltered for half a second. Just a crack.

But then, eyes glassy, voice shaking, "I don't feel safe with you."

I tilted my head, studying her like a puzzle.

"Good. That means I'm getting close." I exhale slowly, keys still twirling between my fingers. "Fine. You don't remember. But humor me, what's the last thing you do remember with Nick?"

Lucy's eyes shift. Then her voice comes out soft, fragile. "He... he said he needed space. That he was scared he'd hurt someone. He didn't even look like himself."

I stared at her, weighing every syllable. It was too neat. But at the same time, it sounded exactly like Nick.

"That's all?" I pressed.

She nodded quickly, too quickly. "That's all I know, I swear."

I pocketed the keys, leaning close enough for her to feel my breath. "See, the problem isn't what you swear. It's what you slip."

Her face tightened, but she didn't falter.

I stood up, letting a long beat pass. I've wasted enough time. Nick's trail was already cold, and Lucy wasn't about to warm it up.

I reached for her, starting a careful search.

"What are you doing?" she asked, confused.

From her pocket, I pulled the note I'd heard her handling earlier. I flashed it in front of her.

"This is why I don't trust you."

"Nick left that for me." she claimed, feigning ignorance.

I opened it. The handwriting was unmistakable. It's from Nick:

The lowest place under the highest sun. Silence louder than cities, heat that burns the ghosts out. No rivers here, only salt and stone. Pray for the road, not for me. The place we whispered of waits for those who remember the edge.

—N

"Dammit, Nick."

The words slipped out before I could stop them.

I glanced at Lucy.

"He's a hell of a writer, but I hate when he pulls this cryptic crap. Why the riddle?" My voice was half to her, half to myself.

Nick's smart. Too smart.

Lucy leaned forward, her tone laced with a flicker of hope. "So... you know where he is, then? What if that note wasn't meant for you at all? What if it was left for me?" Her act almost cracked, but she still clung to it.

I shook my head, pacing, the note clenched in my hand. "I'm not the one in handcuffs, Lucy. This note wasn't for you."

My eyes flicked down to the paper again, scanning it, trying to hear Nick's voice between the lines. The lowest place under the highest sun... the edge... He's clever, but this one was easy.

The note was for me.

Back when we were fresh out of high school, Nick and I had one of those late-night, too-honest talks about the future.

Where life might take us.

How no matter what, we'd have each other's backs. Somewhere in there, the conversation turned dark, what we'd do if things ever got too hard.

I told him if I ever disappeared, I'd probably make it quick. Jump off a bridge, a cliff, something fast, I know it was cliché.

Nick just shook his head. "Not me. I'd be isolated. Go somewhere low, under the sun. Starve it out. Suffer even more before I go."

At the time I thought he was being sarcastic. But it was too strange, too specific. Something I never forgot.

Lucy's watching me now, like she knows, I've pieced it together. Her voice cuts through the memory.

"You okay, Adam?"

I held her stare.

"If this note was meant for you, then tell me, where do you think Nick is?"

"Sounds like he's planning to hit the road," she says, voice measured. "When we were younger, he was fascinated with the Grand Canyon."

I tilted my head at her. "So, you remember that... but not how you ended up in handcuffs?"

"C'mon Adam, we're both worried about Nick's safety, right? We need to work together to figure out where he is, or you know what could happen to him." Lucy's tone was serious, almost pleading.

"So, you've always known?" I pressed.

Her face hardened for a flicker, then softened again.

"Known what? That Nick's not well? Of course. I've been trying to protect him since we were kids."

"I think you're more worried about Clay."

Lucy flinched, just barely, but then shook her head, her eyes wide and soft. "Don't say that. Nick's my friend. I don't care what you think. I just… I just don't want him to hurt himself."

"We'll find Nick together," I said flatly, "but I don't trust you. The cuffs stay on."

"I'm not going to hurt you, Adam. I just want to find him." Her voice trembled, maybe fear, maybe theater.

"You threatened my life last night. You might have 'forgotten' that, but I didn't." I say keeping my eyes on her.

Her gaze darted away. "That wasn't me."

I stiffened. "Then who was it?"

She hesitated, then whispered, "When things get bad, Adam, I just… follow along. I don't fight it. It's the only way I know to keep Nick safe. You think I wanted any of that?"

I don't trust a single word she says. There might be truth behind it, but I'll never admit that to her.

Deep down, I can't shake the thought that maybe I just don't want to believe Nick could be guilty.

"Now you remember. If you were keeping him safe, then why let him poke around C. Holloway? Why suggest that if you already knew?" I say, my voice low, studying her like she's another prisoner.

"What are you talking about?" she says, trying to look innocent again.

"Lucy, stop. I know you know as much as I do," I say, leaned in slightly, watching every micro-expression, waiting for her to crack.

She didn't falter.

"I just… I want Nick to have some kind of closure. He's not handling things well, and I want to support him. That's all."

She wants to play that game, we'll play that game.

Let's see what else she has to say.

"It just sounds to me like you wanted him reading those books. So, tell me, Lucy, how exactly does Nick get closure by realizing he's C. Holloway?" My voice is steady, but the words cut critically. I'm done dancing around it.

"Nick is C. Holloway?" she says, brows knitting like she's genuinely confused.

Was she acting? Or did she not know?

If she's collaborating with Clay, surely, he would've told her. No, Lucy's smart. Too smart. She'd have connected it by now. She's not clueless.

She's playing me.

"Lying to me again?" I snapped. "You're not stupid, Lucy. You read the books; you saw the patterns. You had to put it together. Or…"

I leaned in, eyes locked on hers. My voice dropped, calm and chilling. "Maybe you've known all along. After last night, I'm sure you know more than you're admitting."

Her eyes widened, just for a fraction of a second. Then she blinked, recalibrated, and forced a calmness that didn't reach her eyes. "I… I just want to help Nick. I want him to have closure. Find peace, that's all."

I study her for a long moment, weighing every flicker of expression, every twitch of her hands.

She still didn't flinch.

"Fine," I say finally, straightening. "Whatever you're hiding, we're not getting it out here. Not today." I stepped back, letting the tension hang between us. "We leave in the morning. Until then, you stay put."

I unclipped one cuff and secured her to the thick dining table leg. Solid enough.

Lucy swallowed, a flicker of something, confusion, maybe—flashing across her face. "You know this is illegal, Adam. Goes against everything you stand for."

"What are you going to do? Two options. One, you run and try to report me, but who's going to believe you? Or two, you stay, because deep down, you want to find Clay."

"Correction," she says smoothly. "I want to find Nick. If you know I'm not going anywhere, why the cuffs?"

I didn't answer right away.

Instead, I stepped closer and reached into her jacket pocket. She stiffened, just barely, as my fingers closed around her phone. The screen lit up in my hand.

I powered it off and slipped it into my jacket.

"Because wanting something doesn't mean you get to act on it," I said.

Then I smirked, heading for the kitchen. "Relax. I'll leave you water. Maybe a snack. Hell, I'll even turn on the TV for you."

Her eyes narrowed, "This is paranoia. Inhumane, even."

"Inhumane, sure. But survival comes first. You better pray I'm just being paranoid," I muttered, walking out the door.

***

Outside, the air felt heavier, like the woods were holding its breath. I started going through the list of tasks in my head… coverage at work, gear, tracing Nick's path, but the truth hummed underneath: every wasted hour pulls him further out of reach.

And Lucy? I couldn't trust her. Letting her go would be easy—except every second she's free, she could get to Nick first. That's why she's still cuffed, why I haven't processed her yet. Not an option.

It's almost ten by the time I made it through the woods, boots crunching along the narrow trail that led to my car. Phone in hand, thumb hovering over the screen.

One call before everything else.

It rang twice before a voice picked up.

"Yeah?"

"Captain, it's me." I cleared my throat, keeping my voice even. "I've got a lead I need to chase down. Off the books for now, but it could be connected to Holloway."

Ther was a pause, then a low sigh.

"You asking for time off, or forgiveness later?"

"Both," I admitted. "Give me one week. I'll file the report when I can."

Another pause, longer this time.

Finally, "Fine. But Adam, don't go cowboy. If you're wrong," he said, "you'll answer for it."

"Yes, sir."

I ended the call before he could ask more.

I didn't need to tell my boss about Lucy. Not yet.

Once I did, this wouldn't be mine anymore. It would turn into paperwork, questions, and eyes I wouldn't be ready for.

I needed time, just enough to see where this led.

I slid into the driver's seat, the engine humming under my hands as I pulled onto the road. The miles blurred, but my mind refused to. Questions circled in my head, all of them with Lucy's name attached. Questions I needed answers to, before this spirals out of control.

By the time I pulled into the driveway, a dull pressure pulsed behind my eyes.

My wife was at the counter when I walked in, slicing vegetables for lunch. The smell of garlic and onions grounded me in a way I didn't realize I needed.

"I wasn't sure what time you'd be back," she says, looking up. Her brow furrowed when she caught sight of me. "You okay, hon? What happened to your face?"

I glanced in a mirror, noting the fresh purple bruise along my jaw. "Happened on the job, nothing big. Don't worry, the perp's paying for it."

She stepped closer, her eyes scanning my face.

"You always say that… but I hate seeing you like this. Promise me you'll be careful." She gave me a gentle kiss on my wound and walked back to the cutting board.

I paused, watching her. It was a small lie so she wouldn't worry, but I've always loved that about her—the way she reads me without trying.

She knew what she was signing up for, marrying a detective: long nights, stress, sometimes silence. And still, she never once complained. She knows me almost as well as Nick does.

"It's been a long week," I admitted, setting my keys down. "No time to waste though, I need to run errands. I'll be out of town for maybe a week."

She stopped chopping, knife resting against the board. She's waiting for me to be honest.

"It's Nick," I say finally. "He's not doing well. He left me a note… I've got to track him down before he does something he can't take back."

Her lips pressed into a line, but her eyes soften. Concern, not surprise. "Then be careful. And don't let him do anything stupid." She leaned in and pressed a kiss to my lips, as if that's the last line of defense she can give me.

I smiled, pulling her into my arms, letting myself have the moment. "This is why I married you. How the hell did I get so lucky?"

She laughed under her breath, shaking her head.

"Flattery's not getting you out of this. You're still packing tonight, right?"

"I'll take care of it," I said, though I'm already making a mental list of things I'll probably forget.

"Or..." she says, straightening the collar of my shirt, "since you've got a hundred things on your mind... I'll pack your suitcase for you."

I kissed her forehead, lingering a little longer than I mean to. "I married the best," I murmured, trying to make it sound easy, normal. I stepped back with a lighter tone. "But first, I need a shower. Can you make me lunch to go? Maybe enough for two."

She raised a brow, "For two?"

"Nick's dad," I said, keeping my voice even. "I need to find out where he's at. Maybe he might be with Nick or know where he's headed. Hopefully, that's all it takes."

She studied me for a long moment, like she didn't quite buy it, but then she nodded. "Okay. I'll pack extra. Just… don't let this eat you alive, Adam."

Her words lingered as I stepped into the shower. The hot water did its best to wash the day off, but my mind kept slipping back to Nick's note and that stupid late-night conversation we had when we were kids.

***

I can still see him—eighteen, half-defiant, half-theatrical. We were sitting on the hood of my car, the whole future spread out and stupidly big.

"If I ever hit rock bottom," he said then, "I'd want somewhere that matches it. The Grand Canyon's dramatic, sure—but Death Valley? That's as low as it gets. Imagine being at the planet's belly, where the silence is so loud. No one would find you. You could suffer in peace."

I told him he was being melodramatic. He just stared at the road ahead. "The lowest point in North America, Adam. That's where you'll find me," he'd said, like it was a fact.

Now the lines on that memory blur with the handwriting on the note in my pocket.

Death Valley.

Lowest point.

Wheels.

Silence.

He really meant it.

I'm halfway through toweling off when the phone rang. The number is unfamiliar, but I answered anyway.

"Chaplin speaking."

A familiar voice responded, relief undercut with worry. "Adam... I'm glad you're okay." It's Nick's dad.

"Where are you? Are you with Nick?" I asked, grabbing a fresh shirt as I hurried to get dressed.

"Nick... he's gone," his voice dropped, heavy with disappointment. "I wanted to help him, but he just left."

"Where are you now? I'll come get you," I say, tugging my shoes on with one hand, phone clamped between my ear and shoulder. My pulse is already hammering. "I think I know where he's headed. We need to move fast."

"I'm at the church in Middleton. I'm with Father Bob and—"

I cut him off. I didn't want explanations, not over the phone. "Look, I'll come get you. We'll talk in the car. Just stay put. I'm on my way."

Before he could argue, I hung up. My hands were shaking a little as I grabbed my keys off the counter.

That's when I saw the lunch my wife packed, sitting neatly on the counter, untouched. My throat tightened. She's across the table, eating alone, quiet, pretending not to notice the storm in my head.

"Hon..." I paused, guilt pressing down heavy.

"I'm sorry I can't join you. I'll be back tonight, I promise. We'll spend the evening together before I head out."

She gave me a soft smile, but it didn't reach her eyes. "It's okay. Go. I'll see you later."

I could tell she wanted to ask—what's going on, what aren't you telling me—but she swallowed it, as always.

I leaned down, kissed her lips. "Thank you for lunch, babe. Not sure where I'd be without you."

For a moment, I almost stayed. Almost sat down and told her everything. But instead, I forced myself out the door.

***

The drive to Middleton felt longer than an hour. Every stoplight, every slow car in front of me grated against my nerves. By the time I pulled into the church lot, my knuckles ached from gripping the steering wheel.

Nick's dad was on a bench out front, hunched forward, elbows braced on his knees. He looked smaller somehow, like the weight of it all is finally crushing him. When he saw me, he stood too quickly, tugging at his jacket like he's trying to hold himself together.

He climbed into the passenger seat and exhaled shakily. "I don't know why I thought bringing Nick back here would help. But he took off. I don't know where he went."

"Lucky for you," I say, pulling out of the lot, "I might have an idea. And we'll head out tomorrow."

His hands twisted in his lap. "Adam... it's gotten worse. Clay is weakening him. And even if we find Nick—do you think he'll even want to help himself?"

"Right now, he thinks he's helping himself." My voice hardened without meaning to. "We need to stop him before he does something stupid."

I reached for the lunch bag on the console, forcing a lighter note into the air. I opened it, handed him a burger, and took the other. "My wife packed this. Figured you might be hungry."

The first bite hits like an anchor, grounding me.

Bread, beef, mustard—home.

He looked at the burger in his hands, eyes softening. "Your wife sounds wonderful. Tell her thank you for the meal." He said a prayer and ate a few bites, then glanced at me. "So… you think Nick's going to do something stupid?"

I didn't want to drown him in fear. He's already carrying too much. "We'll find him before it gets to that point," I said firmly. "But first, there's something else we need to manage on the way—Lucy."

His head snapped toward me; surprise flashed across his face. "Lucy! Where is she? I handcuffed her—"

"That was you?" I blurted out. "When I didn't see you around, I figured you might've taken off with Nick, but I wasn't expecting you to cuff her."

"She was working with Clay. I didn't want her running off before talking to you." His jaw tightened.

"Where is she?"

"I left her at the lake house. Safe. After we pick up supplies, I'll take you there. You can stay with her tonight, keep watch. I'm spending the evening with my wife—I'll be back to get you both in the morning."

He nodded, chewing slower now. "So… what did she tell you?"

212

"Not a lot. Just that she claimed she was doing what Clay told her—said it was the only way to protect Nick."

I glanced at him, measuring his reaction. "What do you know about Lucy?"

His expression grew distant.

"She was an odd child. Quiet. Shy. But she and Nick—attached at the hip. I thought it was just kids being kids, but Nick's mom hated it. She started keeping him away from Lucy, saying she wasn't a good friend." His voice dipped, bitter. "I figured it was just hormones or maybe the alcohol talking."

I watched his profile in the passing light, searching for cracks. "Odd how? What made her seem... different?"

"She was shy, maybe too shy. But sometimes she'd cling to Nick like he was the only person in the world. I remember thinking it wasn't normal, the way she'd sulk or get upset if he played with anyone else." He said calmly.

I kept my eyes on the road, feeling the weight of his words. "Sounds like she was... intense," I say carefully, letting him continue.

He nodded slowly. "Looking back, Lucy made it hard for Nick to have any other friends. She...

hovered. Controlled things more than she should have. My wife didn't like it. Said it wasn't healthy."

I glanced at him, trying to reassure him without minimizing his concern. "Nick did fine, though. High school, college... he made it through. He found his own way, even if Lucy was always around."

He let out a small laugh, though it's tinged with worry. "I know, I know. But still... I just want him safe."

I nodded. "We'll find him. And we'll make sure he doesn't get hurt."

After picking up supplies for the week, I drove Nick's dad to the lake house. The afternoon sun glared off the windows as we pulled into the driveway, casting long shadows across the yard.

I killed the engine and stepped out, the gravel crunching under my boots. I moved to the passenger side and opened the door for him.

"Stay here tonight. Keep an eye on her. I'll be back first thing in the morning to pick you both up."

He stepped out slowly, shoulders tense, taking in the house. "I'll make sure she doesn't do anything," he said, voice low but determined.

Slow and careful, he headed inside.

I didn't follow him right away.

Instead, I moved around the property, checking the shed, the small storage closet off the porch, the crawlspace beneath the deck.

Old habits.

I took stock of what was already here and what shouldn't be. A shovel leaning against the wall. A plastic storage bin shoved into a corner. Towels folded and forgotten, damp at the edges. A red gas can tucked behind lawn chemicals, its cap screwed on tight.

Inside the house, Lucy and Nick's dad watched me quietly as I opened cabinets and drawers. Found matches. Duct tape. Ordinary things, harmless on their own.

Together, they weren't.

I made a few quiet decisions when they weren't looking.

By the time I reached my car, the bin was heavier than when we'd arrived. I slid it into the trunk, tucking it beneath an old blanket and a spare jacket, careful to make it look like nothing more than forgotten clutter. I stood there for a moment longer than necessary, hand resting on the lid, as if sealing the thought inside it.

Prepared. Just in case.

I shut the trunk and locked the car.

I went back into the lake house, scanning the room. Lucy hadn't moved. Not a twitch, not a sound. Our eyes met, and for the briefest second, a smirk crossed her face—gone before I could even process it. I didn't trust her. Not for a second. Not yet.

She turned her gaze to Nick's dad, that same perfect innocent expression plastered on. "I'm glad we can find Nick together," she said softly, still playing her part.

I handed him a burn phone. "If anything comes up, call me. Don't hesitate."

Lucy's voice cut through the air. "Wait—if he's staying with me, do I really need these?" She lifted her cuffed hand slightly, eyes wide and pleading.

I smirked, leaning just enough to let her feel my presence. "You tried to kill us last night. How do I know you're not going to try to finish Clay's plan?"

She glanced at Nick's dad, voice almost fragile.

"You've known me since I was a kid. Why would I ever hurt you?"

"I know it's not easy, Lucy," Nick's dad said carefully, voice gentle but firm. "But Adam's right. We can't take the risk."

I stepped back toward the door, watching them both carefully. "I'm leaving now. See you in the morning."

The engine roared to life behind me, carrying me out of the driveway. The sky was darkening, the first hints of night curling over the treetops. Somewhere out there, Nick was moving, running toward who-knows-what, and somehow, I had to be faster.

Before heading home, I made a quick call.

"Yeah. Temporary, supervised travel out of state," I said, keeping my voice low. "He won't be alone. I'll be with him the entire time. Tied to a case."

A pause.

"Beginning of next week. I'll file the paperwork when we're back."

I thought about the lake house—the shed, the storage closet, and the crawlspace beneath the deck. The bin tucked away under blankets, the shovel leaning against the wall, towels stacked in the corner. Matches, gasoline, the trivial things that could matter.

I'd made sure everything was in order earlier, before leaving. Checked. Locked. Ready for anything.

I merged onto the highway, the lake flashing briefly through the trees before disappearing behind the night. I told myself I was just being cautious.

***

The alarm blared at 4 a.m.

It would take about two hours to reach the lake house, and we needed to be on the road as soon as possible if we had any chance of finding Nick in time.

I dressed quickly, moving through the quiet house with practiced efficiency.

My wife stirred when I leaned down to kiss her. Half-awake, she whispered, "Safe travels. See you when you get back."

I nodded, kissed her forehead, and forced a smile I didn't feel.

In the driveway, I loaded the car with everything else we might need for the road trip. The gear didn't weigh as heavy as the thought of Lucy coming with us. Something about it sat wrong in my gut—but for now, it was the only option.

When I reached the lake house, dawn was just brushing pale light across the water. Inside, Lucy lay curled on the floor, cuffed to the table but given a pillow and blanket. The old man wasn't as heartless as I thought. He was snoring on the couch, weathered face slack with exhaustion.

I nudged him awake.

"Come on. Time to move."

Then I crossed to Lucy. She barely stirred until the cuffs clicked open from the table leg.

"Wake up, sleepyhead," I said, crouching beside her.

She blinked groggily—and before the fog of sleep cleared, the cuffs clicked back around her wrists.

"Really, Adam?" she muttered, voice thick with sleep and irritation.

"Still not going to trust you," I said with a half-smile.

Turning to Nick's dad, I asked, "Long night? Hope she wasn't causing any trouble."

He gave me a look—serious, unreadable.

Something had passed between them, something I wasn't sure I wanted to unpack right now. Then he broke eye contact.

"So... what's for breakfast?" he asked, his tone too casual, too quick, like he was dodging the question. Maybe he just didn't want to say anything in front of Lucy. Or maybe he really was just hungry.

Either way, I let it go. "We'll pick something up on the way. I need to get gas anyway. Let's move."

We filed out of the lake house. Nick's dad slid into the passenger seat, Lucy climbing into the back directly behind him. I drove in silence for a while, the weight of the road ahead pressing down on all of us.

At the first gas station, I filled up the tank, then pulled us through a drive-thru for a quick breakfast. It was going to be a long trip.

With food in our stomachs and the road stretching out ahead, Nick's dad broke the silence. "You're not planning to drive straight through, are you? We'll need to stop somewhere if we're heading out west."

I hesitated. The truth was, I had planned to push through—catching Nick before he made it to Death Valley, maybe intercepting him if he pulled off somewhere. But I knew Nick. He wouldn't rush. He'd drag it out, forcing himself to suffer every mile.

The urgency burned in me—I needed to find him as soon as possible. But dragging Lucy into motels posed its own problems. I couldn't risk uncuffing her.

Finally, I forced an even tone. "We'll stop if we need to. I had a long week, and Nick's not exactly speeding his way to Death Valley."

Lucy's voice broke the quiet. "Death Valley? Are you sure he's not heading for the Grand Canyon?" Her tone carried just enough concern to sound convincing.

I caught her eyes in the rearview mirror, narrowing slightly. "Lucy, I don't know about you, but Nick and I had a conversation you probably never had with him. I know where he's going. Death Valley. And if I had to bet—Badwater Basin." As I said it, Nick's words from that night echoed in my mind:

"The lowest point."

She doesn't argue, just offers a faint smile. "I hope you're right."

"Now, Lucy," Nick's dad said carefully, "I know you're friends with Nick too... but on this one, we should trust Adam."

Lucy didn't answer. Instead, her eyes flicked up, catching mine in the rearview mirror. She held the stare just a second too long before looking away again.

A chill crawled up my spine. For someone who barely speaks, she had a way of making silence feel louder than words. I gripped the wheel firmly, forcing myself to focus on the road.

I played music to ease the silence. I couldn't exactly talk about what I wanted in front of Lucy.

After hours of driving, an idea crossed my mind: maybe I could play good cop. She didn't want to answer my questions at the lake house, clearly, walls were up. But I wondered how much she'd reveal on this road trip.

"You know," I said, keeping my eyes on the road, "I'm a little jealous of you, Lucy. You've known Nick longer than I have. I would've loved to know him since I was a kid… maybe even from birth."

She answered quickly, almost too quickly.

"Preschool. It was preschool."

I glanced in the rearview mirror. She was staring out the window, eyes distant, as if recalling the day, she first met Nick.

"So… how did you two become friends?" I asked, trying to keep it light. "Did he share a snack with you or something?" I added with a small laugh, watching for any hint she might slip.

Lucy doesn't answer right away. Her gaze stays fixed on the window, her reflection faint in the glass.

"The other kids didn't want to play with me," she said softly. "They thought I was… strange. Nick didn't. He was the only one who saw me."

She gave a small smile, like she's replaying something tender in her mind. But the way she lingered on "only one" sent a chill down my spine. I couldn't help but wonder what Nick saw in her. Maybe he was just too kind for his own good. Because there's no denying it—Lucy's always been… off.

Off enough that the other kids stayed away.

"Adam, you know Nick means a lot to me," Lucy said, her voice kind, almost fragile. "I'm sorry about the other night, but... you need to believe me. I wasn't myself. I was only doing what Clay told me—because it was the only way to protect Nick. Wouldn't you have done the same?"

"Maybe I would have," I admitted quietly. "But that's not what happened, Lucy."

She leaned back against the seat, her reflection faint in the rearview mirror. "I get it, Adam," she said kindly. "I know Nick will clear things up for me when we see him."

Her calmness twisted my gut.

"Nick or Clay?" I asked, eyes flicking to the horizon, the sun blazing like fire on the mountains.

"Nick." She didn't even hesitate. Like the word itself could shield her from everything. Her voice was steady, but her fingers fidget with the cuffs in her lap. "What are you going to do when you find him?"

I snorted, a short, bitter laugh.

"Drag his ass back home."

Her gaze shifted to the side window, staring at the desert rocks rolling past.

"And then what?" Her voice was quiet, but it cut harder than any yell. "You think that'll fix him? You know the truth... will Nick ever live normally? Or is he destined to suffer with Clay?"

The words hung in the dry, sun-scorched air, heavy and impossible to shake. I glanced in the mirror again, catching her eyes for a split second—calm, unwavering, almost innocent. And yet, I could feel the storm behind them, waiting.

Silence stretched across the miles, broken only by the hum of the tires and the low glow of the sunset bleeding through the windshield. Lucy's words meandered in my mind.

What am I going to do when we find Nick?

Or Clay?

Clay—Nick's other self—was no ordinary threat. He was a ghost in every case I'd read, a name whispered in connection with murders I didn't want to believe. And now Lucy was tangled in it too.

I tightened my grip on the wheel. I couldn't send my best friend to jail... but he needed help. Real help. Medical help, something strong enough to erase Clay before he might hurt anyone else.

Before it was too late.

Several hours slipped by in a blur of gas station stops and greasy takeout wrappers. The radio faded in and out, more static than music, until I finally shut it off. Darkness settled heavier with every mile, and the road felt lonelier than it should have.

It's late. My eyes stung from staring at the endless stretch of headlights and pavement, but I pushed myself to keep going. I didn't trust Lucy enough to sleep.

Still, exhaustion won. When I saw the blue sign for a rest area, I eased off the highway and pulled into the dimly lit lot.

Nick's dad snored softly in the passenger seat, and Lucy—hands cuffed, head tilted against the window—looks almost harmless in sleep. Almost.

I cut the engine and sat there for a moment, listening to the tick of cooling metal.

Rest is dangerous.

But so was driving half-dead.

I closed my eyes for what I promised myself would only be a few minutes, praying Lucy didn't try anything while I was out.

***

I jolt awake with the kind of heaviness that says I'd been out longer than I meant to. The sky's gone gray, and the morning was already pressing in. My first instinct was to check my phone—voicemail, missed calls, something from Nick.

But when I pressed the button, nothing. Black screen. I held it longer.

Still nothing.

Not even a buzz.

Dead.

I frowned, give it a shake like that'd make a difference, but the pit in my gut only sank deeper. I topped off the charge while driving last night on my car charger. No reason it should be dead. Unless—

Unless someone wanted it that way.

From the back seat, Lucy's eyes were open, watching me in the mirror. Too awake. Too alert.

"Phone die on you?" she asked gently, almost like she's relieved.

I cleared my throat, trying to sound casual.

"Guess so. Strange. It was charged."

She shrugged, looking back out the window. The cuffs clinked faintly as she shifted.

"Technology's fickle."

Her tone was light, but my skin was prickling. I know damn well phones don't just die like that.

I didn't say a word. Instead, I reached into the glove compartment and pulled out a second phone, an old backup I keep for cases when things get messy.

The screen lit up at once.

Lucy's eyes flickered in the rearview, before she smoothed her face back into that shy, harmless mask.

"Problem?" She asked faintly.

"Not anymore," I muttered, slipping the dead phone into my jacket and setting the burner on the console.

She doesn't need to know Nick doesn't have this number. He didn't have his phone—and if he did, I couldn't risk Lucy finding a way to contact him.

"Adam, can I use an actual bathroom for once?" Lucy asked, her voice was tender than usual. "I really have to go, and I think I'm on that time of month…"

I glanced at her, trying to read her face. She looked tired, pale even, but I knew better than to take anything she said at face value.

After a beat, I reached into the glove compartment, pulled out my notepad and a pen, and handed them across to her.

"You know what? Fine. But you're writing me a statement first."

Her brows knitted together, feigning confusion.

"I'm not going to run off though. I can do this when I get back?" She tried to smile, innocently.

I let out a short laugh, no humor in it. "You think I care if you run off? I just need something on paper so if you disappear, I don't get my ass handed to me. You don't go anywhere until I've got that."

She stared at the pen in her hand, then at me, like she's deciding whether to argue or cave. The silence stretched long enough to make my skin itch.

Finally, she sighed and lowered her eyes to the page.

Nick's dad stretched in the seat, groaning as his joints pop. "Speaking of, I need to use the restroom myself. I'll be back." He slipped out, letting in a rush of cool morning air before the door thuds shut again.

Lucy keeps scribbling, head bent low. I glanced at her through the rearview mirror as I pulled out the backup phone. My wife has probably been worried sick texting the number that's sitting useless in my pocket. I typed out a quick message, eyes flicking up every few seconds, making sure Lucy's still writing.

She looked calm. Too calm. If I were her, this would be the perfect time to run.

It's just a bathroom, I tell myself. Just a bathroom. And if she does take off... fine. I'll find Nick without her.

Minutes crawl by before Lucy says, "Done." She tore the page free and handed it forward.

"I'll see you soon, Adam."

Her voice was light, almost cheerful, and before I could respond she's already out of the car, her steps were quick toward the building.

Her words sat wrong in my gut.

See you soon.

Not, *"I'll be right back."*

I looked down at the page in my hands—and my blood ran cold. The handwriting. Loops, slants, the same obsessive flourishes. The journal from the lake house. I thought it was Clay's, but it was Lucy's.

Everything tilted sideways, a sick twist curling through me. The car felt too small, too hot, like the air's been sucked out.

Nick's dad climbed back in, slamming the door.

"Lucy in the bathroom?" he asked casually.

I couldn't answer. My eyes are glued to the restroom doors. How long has it been? Five minutes? Ten?

People filtered in and out, none of them are her. My pulse spiked. What if she slipped past me? What if she's already gone?

I shoved the door open and stepped out, scanning the crowd, my heart pounding loud enough to drown everything else.

I'm out of the car before Nick's dad could ask another question, my shoes slapping against the asphalt.

A. Rose

My badge flashed in my hand as I pushed into the women's restroom. A couple of women were at the sinks, startled when they saw me.

"Police," I said quickly, holding the badge high.

"Looking for someone—blonde hair, gray hoodie, looks mid-twenties. Did she come out of here?"

They glanced at each other, then shook their heads. One muttered, "No one else in here but us."

Panic started gripping at my chest. I pushed past the stalls, anyway, swinging each door open.

Empty.

It's then I saw it—folded neatly on the edge of the sink, like she wanted me to find it.

My fingers shook as I unfolded it.

A note, written in that same looping script:

Nice try, Adam. You can't keep me on a leash forever. I'll find Nick first. Don't bother chasing—we both know you'll always be one step behind.

The paper crumpled in my fist before I even realized what I was doing. My jaw clenches, pulse spiking until I could hear it even more in my ears. Then I slammed my fist into the tiled wall, hard enough to rattle the soap dispenser. Pain shot up my knuckles, sudden, grounding.

She's out there now.

Free.

And she thinks I can't stop her.

I stormed back to the car, knuckles still stinging from the wall. Nick's dad looks up, eyes wide.

I glared at him, voice low, sharp. "Are you sure Nick was the one who killed his mom?"

eight

By the time the sun began to sink, the temperature cools. Gold bleeds into purple across the horizon. When I finally reached Badwater Basin, I pulled over.

The place is eerily beautiful. Jagged mountains shadow the vast, barren floor. An emptiness so complete it felt alive.

I parked in the nearly empty lot and climbed out, stretching stiff muscles. Only one other person is there, a woman standing near the railing, staring out at the endless flats. Her long dark hair caught the last light of the sun, falling loose over her shoulders.

"Beautiful, isn't it?" she said without turning. Her voice was calm, almost reverent. I couldn't tell if she was speaking to me or the desert itself.

Still, I answered.

"I definitely underestimated it."

She turned, smiling faintly.

"It's breathtaking. What brings you to the lowest point?"

I paused, unsure if she's making a joke or if she could read me. My throat felt dry, but I manage, "I think I'm supposed to be here."

Her eyes lingered on me, searching.

Then she nodded.

"Me too."

Silence stretched between us, heavy with things neither of us are saying.

She finally stepped closer, offering her hand.

"I'm Lilah."

"Nick," I replied, gripping her hand.

Her gaze held mine, steady and unflinching. There's a brightness in her eyes, like she carries her own light into the desert night, and I couldn't look away.

She tilted her head, smiling. "The sun's dropping fast. Want to walk the trail? It's different once the shadows stretch out, like the desert's showing you another side of itself."

I hesitated, trying to read her. Who asks a stranger that?

She must have caught the doubt on my face because she laughed. "Relax. I travel alone, and I've gotten rather good at trusting my gut. You don't set off any alarms. Besides," her smile edged, "if a mountain lion shows up, you look like the type they'd chase first."

I shook my head, half a smile tugging at my mouth. She's different. Strange, but in a way that didn't push me back, it pulled me in.

Before I could answer, she turned toward the trail, the last slant of sun catching her eyes like fire.

And even though I should stay put, even though a voice deep down whispered I couldn't afford distractions, my feet moved anyway. I followed her.

For the first time in a long while, it didn't feel like Clay, or Lucy, or Adam, or anyone else is steering me.

Just me.

And her.

Walking into the fading light.

The desert air cools fast, carrying that strange stillness you only notice when you're not used to silence. Lilah matched my stride, hands tucked in her jacket, gaze flicking between me and the horizon.

"You're intense, you know that?" she said suddenly.

I glanced at her. "What makes you say that?"

She grinned, "The way you look at everything. Like it's either going to disappear... or kill you."

I laughed under my breath, caught off guard. She's not wrong. "Maybe both," I admit.

Her eyes softened, like she heard more in that, than I said aloud. But she didn't press. Instead, she pointed towards the mountains cut against the pink-and-purple sky. "Most people don't stop long enough to see this. You'd be surprised how many take a picture and just... leave."

I found myself watching her more than the view. She noticed, "What?" she asked, half-smile forming.

I shrugged, pretending it was nothing. "You just... seem like you actually mean what you say."

Her gaze shifted upward. "When you've lost enough, you learn to pay attention to what's left."

For a moment, I wanted to tell her everything. About Adam. About Lucy. About Clay. The words hovered, but I locked them down. Instead, I just said:

"Yeah. I get that."

We stopped where the trail opened wide, the sun sliding behind the ridge. Lilah tilted her head back, eyes tracing the first stars. "Crazy, isn't it? We're standing at the lowest point on the continent, and the whole universe is right there above us."

I should feel small. Broken. But walking beside her, for the first time in a long time, I felt like maybe I'm not completely lost.

"You're not taking off anywhere, are you?" Lilah asked, tilting her head at me, eyes searching like she'd really be disappointed if I left. "The sky's clear tonight. Stars are going to blanket the whole basin. No light pollution, no noise... just us and the universe."

Her words spilled quickly, then she bit her lip like she realized she's been rambling.

"Really?" I asked, surprised at myself for meaning it. For the first time in days, I could breathe.

"Let's watch the sky then."

Her face lit up. She jumped, like a kid tearing into a gift. "Yes! This is perfect." Her excitement was contagious; I couldn't stop the small laugh that slipped out of me.

As we headed back towards the parking lot, her voice danced ahead of us. "I've got blankets and an air mattress we can set up in the bed of my truck. We'll spread out, eat snacks, and let the stars do the heavy lifting."

Her eyes caught the last of the light, glowing like they belong to another world entirely. So alive it made something in my ribs ache, a reminder of how long I've been stuck in the shadows. And without even trying, she's pulling me out of them.

I didn't know why, but I felt tethered to her already, like the desert itself pushed us together.

Back in the parking lot, I helped her spread blankets across the bed of her truck, then headed to my RV to grab extra snacks. She hummed aimlessly as she worked, half-singing pieces of a song I recognized. Her voice drifted through the cooling air, easy and unguarded.

She's different. She didn't even have to try and somehow, that's what drew me closer.

We climbed into the bed of her truck and sank into the blankets, the night sky slowly blooming above us, stars flickering to life one by one. She pulled out a blunt, flicked her lighter, and took a hit that instantly made her cough.

"Would you like to partake?" she asked in an exaggerated British accent, her voice raspy from the smoke.

I laughed, taking it from her. "Well, don't mind if I do," I replied, matching her accent as I inhaled.

She laughed again—light, unguarded and something about the sound made my heart feel weightless.

We passed the blunt back and forth, smoke curling up into the growing dark. The air between us hummed with something easy, something real.

She turned her head toward me. "Do you ever feel like… you meet certain people at the exact moment you're supposed to?"

I glanced over, surprised. "You mean like fate?"

She shrugged, smiling faintly. "Maybe. Or maybe it's just timing. Some people show up when you need them, even if you don't realize why yet."

I thought about that, about her, and the weight in my chest dissipated.

"You sound like someone who believes everything happens for a reason."

"So, what if I do?" she said. "But I like to think the good things do. And sometimes… The bad ones can turn into good things too. Depends on how you look at it."

We fell silent again, our shoulders barely brushing. The stars multiplied above us, scattered like diamonds across an endless dark.

She tilted her head back. "You ever think about how stars are just… reminders?"

"Reminders of what?" I asked.

"That even after they die, their light still travels. For thousands of years." She smiled gently. "I guess that's why I like them. They're proof that something beautiful can outlive its own ending."

I glanced at her, the glow from her phone screen barely lighting her face.

"That's kind of sad."

She shook her head. "Maybe. Or maybe it's faith. Like in the Bible—how the wise men followed a star to find something greater. Maybe that's all we're ever doing, really. Following little bits of light in the dark, hoping they lead somewhere."

There was something in the way she said it that lodged deep in my core. The wind moved through the desert like a sigh.

"You believe in God?" I asked.

"I believe in a lot of things," she said, eyes still fixed on the sky. "And I most definitely believe in God." She paused for a moment.

"I just don't think He lives in buildings or prayers. I think He hides in little moments—the way the stars burn for us, or the way someone shows up when you need them most." Her voice dipped lower. "I don't think we ever really die, either. I think we just… go back to the light."

The way she said it made me hold my breath. Maybe because part of me wanted to believe it too. Maybe because I've seen too much darkness to think there's nothing left after.

I glanced up at the stars, and for a moment, they didn't feel like distant suns, they felt like witnesses. Each flicker above seemed to echo what she just said, like the universe itself agreed with her.

Her words about the light, about going back to it, settled something within me. I felt it stirring— warm, strange, almost like hope. Or maybe it's just the way she looked at the sky, so certain, so alive, that it made the dark feel… safe.

I shifted closer to her on the bed of her truck without thinking. "You make the dark feel… easier to breathe in," I said quietly.

She turned her head slightly, catching my glance, a small smile tugging at the corners of her lips. "That's the best compliment anyone's ever given me," she said sincerely.

And just like that, the deserts night didn't feel so lonely anymore.

A shooting star streaked across the sky, bright and fast. "A shooting star! Did you see that?" I asked, excitement simmering in my voice.

She frowned, disappointed. "What? I missed it! You better make a wish. I'm not missing the next one."

Her eyes stayed glued to the heavens as she dug into the snacks, opening them and nibbling absentmindedly, completely captivated by the stars.

I watched the sky as the streak of light fades.

A wish.

I paused, wondering what I could even wish for. "I wish…"

"Don't say it out loud!" Lilah interrupted, eyes wide and serious. "It won't come true if I hear it."

I bit back a smile and stayed quiet, letting the thought sit just for me. Another shooting star blazed across the horizon.

"Lilah! You must have seen that one!" I exclaimed.

She pouted, turning toward me like it's the world's greatest tragedy. "I swear I looked away at the wrong time! I need to see one tonight," she says, glancing back at the sky, eyes glued to the stars. "I want to make my wish too…"

I chuckled at her intensity, the way she's completely caught up in the magic of the moment. It's as if the weight I'd been carrying felt lighter too.

The desert night stretched endlessly around us. "You'll get your star," I said. "Just keep watching, don't look away this time."

She flashed me a grin, one corner of her mouth tugging up like she's in on a secret. "Fine. But if I miss it again, I'm blaming you."

I watched her for a moment, and I felt that strange warmth again—the one that made the dark feel easier to breathe in. In that moment, none of the chaos, none of the danger, exists.

Just the stars, the desert, and her.

Another streak illuminated across the sky.

"There!" I pointed.

She gasped, eyes wide, and for a moment I swear she looked like a little kid seeing fireworks for the first time.

"Did you make a wish?" I asked, curious, but careful not to push.

She glanced at me, her smile softening. "Always," she whispered, her voice almost swallowed by the night.

And just like that, I felt myself leaning closer without even realizing it, drawn in by her laughter, her light, her presence.

Lilah tilted her head, eyes bright in the moonlight. "You know," she began, "shooting stars aren't just pretty streaks across the sky. They're supposed to mean something—hope, change, new beginnings... or maybe a little luck if you believe in that sort of thing." She looked at me, a smile playing on her lips.

"When I see one, I like to think it's a reminder. That even in the darkness, there's a spark for something good to happen."

I swallowed, watching her hands brush against the blankets as she adjusted them. "That's... nice," I say quietly, feeling some of the tension I'd been carrying ease just by hearing her.

Her smile deepened. "So, when you see one," she adds, "you don't just make a wish. You remember that something beautiful can still appear, even when it seems impossible."

Another streak of light cut across the sky.

"Did you see that one?" I whispered, pointing.

"Another one!" she said excitedly.

She closed her eyes for a moment, making another wish quietly to herself. I watched her as her eyes opened, like she knows there's something fragile about this night that needed protection. Without thinking I reached out gently, brushing a loose strand of hair behind her ear.

She shivered slightly, and then smiled, nestling a little closer. I felt the warmth of her shoulder against mine, the steady rhythm of her breathing as we settled onto the blankets.

We talked in whispers about everything and nothing—the desert, the stars, freedom, what could be. Each word drifted into the night air, light enough that it felt like the wind might carry it away. The world around us was quiet. Flat white salt stretched for miles in every direction; the stars scattered above like spilled glass.

Lilah lay next to me in the bed of her truck, her hair fanned out against the blanket beneath us. The air was cool, dry, and still. She hummed between words, almost like she's harmonizing with the night. For the first time in years, I felt my body unclench.

"You know," I said, smiling faintly, "this road trip's been pretty insane so far."

She turned her head toward me, her eyes catching the starlight. "How so?"

I let out a short laugh. "Back in Utah, I ran into this hippie at Angel Point. He gave me these chocolates—said they'd help me 'see things differently.' Didn't tell me they were magic mushrooms until after I ate them."

Lilah laughed quietly, the sound small and genuine.

"Yeah," I continued, "I thought it'd just be a fun high. But something about that trip... I don't know. It cracked something open. My life's been a mess, and I think for the first time, I saw it for what it was. I'm still trying to process it, but I feel lighter than I did days ago."

She didn't ask questions. Didn't pry. Just listened—her gaze fixed somewhere beyond the stars.

After a while, she says, "I've read that shrooms can do that. They don't fix you, they just show you what's already broken. When I tripped once, I felt like I could see everything. The world above me, the weight below me. It was terrifying... but freeing."

Her voice carried easily in the open air, calm and steady. She looked at me then, her expression thoughtful. "I'm glad it pulled you out of whatever darkness you were in. Even in the dark, light endures. The dark can swallow everything else, but never the promise of light."

She paused, looking past me at the horizon.

"And if you ever find yourself lost in a room without a single spark—look closer. The light wasn't ever missing..."

Her lips curved into the faintest smile.

"...It was you."

The words sank into me like the desert cold—intense at first, then strangely comforting. Something in me shifted, quiet and certain, like she just pieced together something I didn't realize was broken.

The desert fell silent. The stars kept burning above us, reflected faintly on the truck's metal edges. The night felt endless, but not empty.

After a while, Lilah shifted closer, her shoulder brushing mine. I draped an arm around her, and she settled against my chest, warm and steady. Her breath slowed, matching mine.

The salt flats shimmered faintly under the moonlight, and I realized this is the calmest I've felt in a long, long time. Just the two of us—open sky, chilly air, and the kind of peace that made the world feel almost right.

The night deepened, the desert around us was quiet except for the faint rustle of wind. I traced idle patterns on her arm, feeling the comfort of this fleeting moment, knowing I might never feel so safe again.

And then, under the vast, star-filled sky, we drifted off to sleep together in the bed of her truck, hearts quietly beating in rhythm with the universe around us.

***

I woke up to the distant hum of a car door shutting and footsteps crunching on salt flats. The sky was still dark. Lilah shifted next to me, pulling a thin blanket tighter around her shoulders.

For a moment I forgot where I was—until I realized the parking lot lights were dim, distant, and the only sound was whispering wind. I glanced over at Lilah, and she met my eyes, half asleep, the corners pulled into a sleepy smile. We looked at each other at the same time and started laughing like we were teenagers that did something we weren't supposed to be doing.

Lilah stretched her arms toward the sky, her hair wild and tangled from sleep.

"Guess we survived the night," she says, still smiling. "And no mountain lions."

"Yeah," I said, rubbing my neck. "Though I'm not sure my back did."

She laughed again, that bright kind of laugh that made the world feel less heavy. "That's what I get for falling asleep on a stranger in the middle of the desert."

"Technically," I said, smirking, "we're friends now. We shared snacks and existential thoughts. That's like, level two friendship."

"Level two?" She tossed a chip bag at me, "What's level three?"

"I think that's when you let someone make you coffee."

She gasped dramatically. "Oh, dangerous territory."

But she's already reaching into her truck bed for a small camping stove. The smell of coffee filled the dry air, earthy and grounding. We sat on the edge of the truck bed, watching the horizon turn gold.

For a while, neither of us talked.

The silence was easy.

Then Lilah said, "You ever feel like the world just… hits pause? Like right now—it's too still to be real."

I glanced at her. "Maybe it's giving us a break. We probably needed one."

She nodded, staring into her mug. "I think so too. Sometimes you don't realize all the noise you've been carrying until it's quiet again."

Something about the way she said that felt like she's talking about more than noise.

***

By noon, the sun was brutal again. We drove out toward the Mesquite Dunes. Lilah climbed the ridges like a kid, arms out, laughing as the wind whipped through her hair. I trailed behind her, half in awe, half out of breath.

When she finally stopped at the top, she looked down at the endless waves of sand. "You know what's funny?" she says. "Everyone thinks deserts are empty. But they're not. They just don't show you everything at once."

I blinked at her, the wind carrying her words.

"You talk like someone who's seen too much."

"Maybe I have," she said, half-smiling. "But I still think beauty wins sometimes."

We hike far enough into the dunes that the world turned into nothing but waves of gold. The sand crunched beneath our shoes, the wind carrying the dry scent of heat and distance.

My eyes squinted against the glare.

"You're seriously setting up a picnic out here?"

Lilah grinned, dropping her bag onto the slope of a dune. "Of course. Who picnics in a desert? That's exactly why we should."

I shook my head, though a small laugh escaped.

"You're out of your mind."

"Maybe. But at least it's a creative kind of madness."

She spread out a blanket that flapped like it's trying to flee the scene. She fought with it, laughing as sand clung to everything. I finally gave in and helped, pinning one side down with my shoe.

"See?" she says, breathless but smiling.

"Teamwork."

I dropped beside her, still half in disbelief. "This has to be the least practical meal I've ever had."

She opened a container of strawberries and handed me one. "Good. Practical is boring."

We sat for a while, just listening to the wind sweep across the dunes, getting sand blown into our sandwiches. The sky burned pale blue above us, fading into white near the horizon.

"So," I say after a moment, "you do this kind of thing often? Picnics in the middle of nowhere?"

"Sometimes," she said. "I like seeing the world from places no one thinks to stop." She glanced at me, her tone softening. "I'm kind of... an artist. I take photos, paint sometimes, and write when I can't sleep. I guess I just try to make things out of what's left."

"What's left?" I repeated it quietly.

She shrugged. "Life, mostly. Pieces of myself to leave behind." Then she smiled again, as if she brushed away something heavier than she wanted to admit.

"Actually, wait." She rummaged in her bag and pulled out a battered old film camera.

My brow arched, "You still use one of those?"

"Digital's too clean," she said, adjusting the lens. "Film makes everything feel more real. You only get one shot, you know?"

She looked at me suddenly. "Smile."

I blinked. "What?"

"Come on. You can't sit in the desert with me and not take a picture."

I hesitated for a moment then sighed. "Fine."

She lets out a light joke, "What, are you wanted for murder or something?"

Lilah slid closer, the corner of her arm brushing mine. The camera clicked—mechanical and final. She lowered it and looked at the viewfinder, a satisfied grin tugging at her lips. "Perfect. You look like you're pretending to be miserable."

I smirked, "That's probably accurate."

"Good," she said, slipping the camera back into her bag.

"Real moments only."

I glanced at her, at the way sunlight glowed against her eyes, her hair. How she smiles like she's trying to memorize the moment herself. "Guess that's your thing, huh? Catching real moments?"

Her eyes lingered on me for a beat longer than I expected. "Yeah," she says quietly, "before they disappear."

We drove for a while, the world outside shifting from dusty gold to deep amber. Lilah's got her camera in her lap, snapping photos through the window, half of them probably blurred, but she didn't seem to care.

Lilah's eyes followed the horizon. "I used to think I had to make something out of the pain I carried. Like if I didn't, it'd eat me alive. But lately… I've been trying to just be. You know? Not dwelling on what's behind me, not rushing what's ahead. Just the present."

Her tone stilled me. She's calm, grounded—but there's something behind her words. A shadow she refuses to let out.

The sun slanted low through the windshield, casting streaks of gold across the dashboard. Lilah's long hair caught the light, every strand glowing like it's on fire. I watched her longer than I should have before smiling.

"You seem like you've lived a few lifetimes," I say.

She laughs quietly; eyes still fixed on the road ahead. "Maybe I have," the corners of her mouth lifting. "But I think this one's my favorite so far."

She shifted in her seat to grab something from her bag, but the zipper caught. A second later, a handful of pill bottles tumbled onto the floorboard, clattering against the metal.

Her body stiffened.

"Shit—sorry," she muttered, quickly leaning down to scoop them up.

I glanced away, pretending to focus on the road, giving her space.

She exhaled sharply, trying to force a laugh.

"Don't worry, I stopped taking most of them. Only use the pain meds when it gets bad."

She tucked the bottles away, cheeks flushed.

I kept my tone soft, careful. "Lilah, you don't have to talk about it if you don't want to." I glanced at her, catching the reflection of the sunlight in her eyes. "I get it."

For a long moment, the only sound is the hum of the tires against the asphalt.

She kept her gaze out the window, her voice was small when it finally came.

"The doctors gave me less than a year to live."

The words hit like a punch, quiet but absolute. My hands clamped down on the wheel.

"Lilah…" I breathed, searching for something to say. "I'm so sorry—"

She shook her head quickly, cutting me off.

"Don't be, Nick." Her voice trembled, but there's a calm in her eyes. She wiped away a tear before it could fall. "It's not like I've given up. I just... decided I'd rather live the time I have than count down what's left."

The sunlight flickered through the passing desert, painting her in gold again.

She hesitated, her gaze drifting toward the horizon. "And I'll get to see my family soon again," she says quietly. "They died in a car accident when I was ten. Survivor's guilt doesn't really go away."

A breath of silence passed between us, filled only by the hum of the road.

"When He decides to take me," she continued, looking up at the sky, "I'll have stories to share with Him. Good ones. I'll also have stories that I've left behind."

She smiled—small at first, then brighter, like she's trying to convince both of us that it's okay.

"I can't wait to tell Him about you."

Something twisted in my chest. The road stretches endlessly ahead, but for the first time, it felt too short.

How could someone so positive, so alive, be hiding all that darkness?

***

By the time we made it back to Badwater, the sky is streaked with pink and orange again.

Lilah pulled a folded blanket from the back seat and spread it across the bed of her truck. The fabric fluttered in the warm wind before settling.

"Are you waiting for someone?" she asked. "Not a lot of people stick around out here this long."

"Yeah," I admitted, my voice lowered. "My best friend. But… I'm not sure if he's coming. Or if he's even okay."

She paused; concern flickered across her face.

"I'd let you use my phone to try and reach him, but there's no service for miles. We could've looked for service earlier instead."

"It's okay," I added quickly. "I called him and left him a voicemail. I'll give him another day to get here."

My eyes are fixed on the empty stretch of desert. The sun sank lower, spilling gold and red across the salt flats. The wind hummed low, carrying that strange, lonely kind of quiet that makes you realize how small you really are.

I started to think back on what she shared with me earlier, how she was so open with me in that moment, about her life. Maybe I should tell her about how messed up mine has been.

255

Then Lilah smiled faintly and says, "You know, I used to be afraid of sunsets. I thought they meant endings. Now I think they're just reminders that beautiful things don't last forever, but they're worth watching anyway."

I glanced at her, "You always talk like that?"

She shrugged, playfully again. "Only when I'm with people who listen. Otherwise, the thoughts just stick in my head."

We both laughed.

The last of the light faded, and I felt it—peace, fleeting and fragile. Like the desert's holding its breath for what comes next.

Time passed quietly between the laughter and conversations. We talked for hours more. Neither of us could sleep, so we decided to go for a late-night walk along the basin trail.

Lilah was laughing, a sound that felt like it be-longed to another world. "You know, Nick, you really don't belong in a place this boring. The desert could use your sarcasm," she teased, nudging me lightly.

I grinned, feeling warmth creeping into my chest I hadn't known I'd needed. "Guess I'm lucky you brought a little light into my life," I said, letting my-self relax.

She reached for a snack in her bag, "Staying positive is my specialty," she said with a sly smile.

***

I swallowed hard, the words clawing their way out. "Lilah... I should've told you everything. About my friend—Adam, about... about what's been happening. I—I didn't mean for any of it to get this out of control."

Her eyes flicked to me, patient, waiting. I swallowed again, starting to ramble.

"Lucy... she's not like anyone I've ever met. She was a childhood friend... but she's—she's unstable, dangerous. Sometimes I blackout—forgetting— thinking everything was my fault. I tried to—"

And before I could finish, before Lilah could say anything, a movement too fast to process slammed into the edge of my vision.

Lucy was there, out of nowhere, her eyes wild. The glint of metal caught the moon's glow before I even realized what was happening.

"Lilah—"

My voice broke as I lunged forward, but it was too late.

Lilah was on the ground, her hand pressed weakly against her neck, crimson spilling through her fingers soaking the white basin floor. I dropped beside her, pulling her into my arms, my heart breaking all over again.

Her eyes found mine, like she was still trying to comfort me. "Nick... the stars heard my wish," she whispered, a faint smile ghosting her lips.

I shook my head, gripping her tighter. "No, you can't go. Not like this."

She coughed, a streak of red staining her chin, but somehow—somehow—she still smiled.

"It's in His plan," she breathed.

"I'll see you in the stars... and if there's a next life," her voice faltered, her eyelids fluttering. "Find me sooner, so we get more time."

"Lilah, please—"

But her body went still.

And just like that, the world was silent again.

Time slowed.

The air vanished in my chest.

My hands were frozen.

Clay hissed inside my mind. *Let me take over. You can't stop this on your own.*

No.

Not this time.

I pushed the cold weight of him aside, shoved the horror aside, and acted. I slammed Lucy to the ground, holding on as if letting go would make everything fall apart. She laid there, still, her eyes wide, watching me but not struggling.

My lungs heaved, adrenaline screaming through my veins, and for a moment I couldn't tell if she was scared—or just waiting.

She locked eyes with me, her voice soft and dangerous. "Nick… let's get away together. We don't need anyone else—"

"No! Lucy, what the fuck did you do?" I yelled, rage burning in my core, my voice raw.

"I love you, Nick…" she whispered, like that could make it all okay.

Her words made my heart coil.

Her love wouldn't fix this.

Not ever.

"I don't want your love, Lucy," I hissed, staring straight into her eyes as I pinned her down. "You framed my dad. You killed people close to me—people who didn't deserve to die. I will never love you."

Her gaze never wavered, her voice almost tender. "If you won't see it now," she whispered, fingers inching toward the knife, "we'll just finish this life and start the next one together."

"Lucy, stop!"

My dad's voice cut through the chaos.

And in one brutal instant, he lunged between us.

The knife sank into him instead of me.

Time broke.

My stomach dropped even lower; my heart thundered against my ribs.

"No!"

I screamed, raw and guttural, as my dad's knees buckled beneath him.

"Dad! Stay with me!"

Warm blood slicked my hands as I held him, my vision blurring with panic.

"Stay away! Stay the hell away!" I roared at Lucy, shoving her aside. In that instant, I realized I wasn't Clay. I was me, and this time, I wouldn't let either of them win.

"I'm not starting anything new with you, Lucy—not here, not after death, not even in Hell."

My dad groaned, his strength failing, blood soaking through his shirt. He managed a faint, trembling smile, locking eyes with me.

"Nick... live," he rasped, voice breaking. "Don't let her win... I can see her now, your mom. She looks so beautiful... like the day I met her." His eyes flickered, with something far away. "She says it's time to go... We love you, son."

I pressed my hands to the wound, trying to stop the flow, hearing only the frantic thud of my own pulse.

Adam had tackled Lucy; she didn't struggle. She only looked at me, smiling like a blade.

"You'll come back to me, Nick. You always do."

Her voice landed like ice. Something inside me cracked—a soundless fracture that turned numbness into motion.

No more.

Not another life.

Not another name.

I guess this is the end of our story. Clay whispered in my head, just for a heartbeat.

My fingers closed around the knife half-buried in the sand. I don't remember deciding to do it, only the weight in my hand and the roll call of faces in my mind.

I drove the blade into her once, "For my mom." Then again, "For Claire." My voice shredded as it left my throat.

Another plunge.

"For Jessica."

Another.

"For Clara."

The strikes came hot and ugly, a litany of everything she'd stolen.

I plunged again, deeper.

"This one's for Lilah."

And the last one went deepest.

"For my dad and I—for the life you took from us."

When I stopped, the world narrowed to the ragged sound of my breathing and a stunned, hungry silence that rolled into the dark. I could still feel the knife's weight in my hand and the hot, terrible list of names echoing in my skull.

Adam stood frozen for a second, watching me like he was trying to decide which part of this was real. Then he moved with cop-quiet efficiency I'd seen a hundred times in the movies: to his car, back again with a duffel and rolls of plastic, which he dropped onto the sand without a word.

"I can't call it in," he said flatly, voice small against the emptiness. "Not yet. We get Lucy somewhere clean, then I'll call it in." He didn't look at me when he said it, only at the body at my feet.

"We don't make this about emotion," he continued. "We document. We stick to the story. We control what goes out." He spoke like a man who'd learned to move the narrative before it moved him.

"A story?" I asked. My voice sounded small and foreign.

"A simple one." He gave me a look that was equal police officer and conspirator. "It was her; she left the scene. She's missing. We give them traces, leads. We keep you out of anything public for a while. The less you show, the less they pry."

The desert had a way of making decisions look smaller and sharper at the same time. "And when someone asks?" I spoke.

"We tell them the truth we can live with," Adam said. "The kind that keeps you alive."

He paused then, and for the first time I saw something flicker behind his calm, not pity, but sorrow.

We didn't say another word as we bagged Lucy's body and wiped away what was left of her from the salt flats. The silence between us felt heavier than the night itself. A few cars passed in the distance, headlights sweeping across the basin. We froze each time until they were gone, praying no one decided to stop.

When it was done, we left my dad and Lilah as they were. Adam and I lifted Lucy's body into the trunk of his car, along with everything else that needed to disappear.

He looked at me as he slammed the trunk shut, eyes steady but full of weight. "You want to do this," he asked quietly, "or should I?"

The desert was quiet again. Too quiet. My hands shook as I couldn't look away from my dad or Lilah lying on the ground. Adam didn't say much, he just looked at me with this understanding that words couldn't touch.

"I'll handle it," he said finally.

I knew what he meant. I didn't ask where he'd take her, or how he'd make it all disappear. Maybe I didn't want to know. I just stood there, between two lifeless bodies and a night sky that looked too beautiful for what had happened below it.

nine

I motioned toward the small pile of clothes I'd grabbed from the car. "Nick, I need your clothes. Come on, let's get you cleaned up a bit." My voice tried to stay calm, but even I could feel the edges of panic in the pit of my gut.

He looked at me, eyes wide and hollow.

"Cleaned up? After... after what?"

I crouched slightly, keeping my tone firm but gentle. "I know it's messed up. I know it's... wrong. But the clothes you're wearing now have Lucy's blood on them. If anyone checks the scene, the story won't line up. We need this to make sense. Just trust me."

He hesitated, trembling.

"And... you want me to...?"

I nodded, swallowing.

"Yeah. After you get changed, I need you to hold your friend and your dad again. Just like we rehearsed. Their blood, your story—it needs to match what you're telling detectives."

He flinched at the words, and I could see the horror flicker in his eyes.

"You mean… hug them again?"

I let out a slow breath, trying to steady the tremor in my voice. "I know it sounds fucked up because it is. I hate that I'm asking you to do this. But it's the only way to keep the story straight. For you, for them, for what really happened."

He stared at the blood-dark stains on the shirt in his hands, knuckles white. Fear and confusion warred with that stubborn little impulse to trust me.

Finally, he swallowed and nodded. "I… okay. I'll do it. For them." His voice cracked on the last word—softer, like a prayer.

Then, as if remembering something fragile, he added, "Her name was Lilah, by the way. Her soul was—"

He choked on the rest.

"—beautiful. Bright. And my dad—I didn't even get the chance to tell him I'm sorry…"

The words hit like a quiet thunderclap. I let out a slow breath. "I'm sorry about Lilah… and your dad." My hand stayed on his shoulder, light but firm.

"But you still got me, we do this together. Step by step. You're not alone in this."

He looked up at me then, and for a moment I saw the kid I'd known for years—not the vacant man the desert had almost carved out of him.

He drew in a ragged breath, trying to steady his shaking hands. He swallowed hard, his jaw tight.

"It's just... too much. I don't know if I can..." His voice cracked, and I could see the panic in his eyes, the weight of everything pressing down on him.

"Nick," I said firmly, squeezing his shoulder, "this isn't the time to hesitate. I need to leave and call this in, and I'm not letting you go to prison for this. You hear me?"

He nodded and we got into his RV, shoulders trembling. He hurriedly and carefully peeled off his bloodied clothes.

I grabbed some towels, carefully pouring bleach onto it, my hands steady despite the tension coiling in my gut. I wiped down his hands, any area on him with blood, careful not to spill a drop. The strong scent fills the small space between us.

"Here," I said, handing him hand sanitizer, then a small squirt of lotion. "And clean clothes."

He eyed the fresh set warily. "Where'd you get these?"

"I came prepared," I said, trying to keep my voice light, though my stomach felt tense.

He slipped into the fresh set of clothes, fidgeting with the fabric, and I could see the strain in his movements.

We both looked back out at the scene through the RV window. The desert stretched endlessly, through the darkness. Shadows from the rocks still lingered, like ghosts of what had happened.

I exhaled slowly.

"I'm sorry, Nick... but you know you have to."

He closed his eyes for a moment, then nodded again, as if steeling himself, gripping the edge of the seat. I could feel the dread radiating off him—fear, grief, and disbelief all tangled together. And I knew there was no turning back now.

I watched him tremble as he held onto them, just like he had earlier. The quiet sobs, the panic twisting through his body, it cut through me, making the air feel trapped in my lungs. I couldn't look away, even though every instinct told me to.

When he finally came walking back, his eyes were drained—not the vacant control of Clay, but something heavier, raw. Someone finally facing the weight of what he had felt all along.

"I'll be back," I said, voice low. "Hang in there and make sure no one tampers with the scene. If anyone stops, tell them I'm already calling it in."

"Wait... what if someone sees? What if—" He stopped, swallowed hard, and shook his head. "I'll... I'll keep it together. For you. For them."

***

I got into my car, pressing both hands onto the wheel and muttered under my breath,

"Fuck. What the fuck."

Then I stomped the gas, as if speed could erase the night. The road blurred beneath the headlights. The desert stretched endlessly on either side, empty and unforgiving.

There was no destination, only the need to put distance between me and Badwater Basin—far enough to think, close enough to return before anyone stumbled across them.

Dust swirled around the car as I drove, the world outside turning hollow and unfamiliar. The asphalt gave way to washes of stone and sand, the landscape shifting in the pale glow of my headlights. I gritted my teeth and kept going, the enormity of what had just happened closing down on me with every mile.

When I finally stopped, the engine turned off like a rumor. The night was a physical thing—a cold so dry it crawled under my skin.

I opened the trunk with numb fingers and hauled the bag out because my mind had gone to autopilot and autopilot follows the only script it knows. I carried her like a thing that didn't belong to me, like a secret I'd been handed and couldn't refuse.

I removed the bag and set her down beside a cluster of wind-smoothed boulders. The moon was a pale coin, and it made everything sharp: the line of her cheek, the dark spread on her clothes.

"You brought this on yourself," I said, because the silence felt like an accusation if I didn't. I told myself it was for Nick, but the words tasted like bile.

The ground around the rocks whispered under something's tread. At first, I thought it was the wind, then the sound resolved into a low, almost velvet purr.

A pair of yellow eyes blinked at me from the shadow and then the animal moved—sleek, indifferent, a shape that belonged to this raw place.

A mountain lion, drawn by scent.

It slipped forward without sound and then, with a casual horror that felt like fate, began to feed.

Everything narrowed down to that: the animal's quiet, efficient movements, the wet sound of flesh, the way night swallowed the rest.

I wanted to look away, to run and undo, to pull her back and make the world right again, but my feet were led. I stood there and watched like I was watching someone else's life, caught in the thin line between action and consequence.

When I had enough of looking, I moved backward on my feet, I could barely keep steady. I didn't approach. I didn't try to compete with an animal that had no concept of guilt.

I got in the car and finally exhaled, a sound that felt at once enormous and small.

My brain raced, assembling excuses, possibilities, anything to put a lid over what I'd done. If the police ever traced her to this place—if they ever found bones or fragments, they'd have explanations.

They'd find reasons.

They always did.

That thought steadied me in an ugly way: if the earth or a wild thing could erase the immediacy of the scene, maybe the rest could be made to look like something else entirely.

I didn't let the logic sit for long. Logic was a dangerous thing tonight. Guilt was not something you could think away, it sat on my ribs and hammered. I started the car, listening to it thrumming like a second heartbeat, and drove back toward town with the desert swallowing my taillights.

The drive back from the rocks was a blur of headlights and static. My hands were stiff on the wheel, every muscle locked. I kept seeing her face, the slack jaw, the way the light caught her eyes before the mountain lion moved in.

I hadn't buried her.

Didn't have to.

The desert had its own way of cleaning up after monsters.

By the time I hit the main road, a faint bar of service flickered to life on my phone. I pulled over, hands shaking as I dialed. The call connected—thin, crackling.

"This is Detective Adam Chaplin," I said, keeping my voice steady. "Requesting immediate dispatch to Badwater Basin. Two confirmed deceased. One male, one female. Suspect fled the scene on foot—white female, appears to be mid to late twenties. Last seen heading east. No vehicle."

I gave them coordinates and ended the call before they could start asking questions.

The story was set.

The facts they'd find would fit—blood, bodies, chaos. Lucy would be gone, and by morning, the desert would already be erasing her.

I took a breath, then made the second call.

My supervisor.

"Yeah... it's me," I said when the line picked up, my voice kept controlled. "I just made a report to dispatch."

I could hear the faint shuffle of papers, the murmur of voices in the background. I clutched the steering wheel.

"Two confirmed homicides," I continued.

"Location—Badwater Basin. Victims: one male, one female. Suspect still at large."

A pause stretched between us, heavy.

"You're going to want to pull the full case files on C. Holloway," I said finally. "This is her."

Another pause. Static hummed softly between words.

"No," I said quietly. "You don't know the full extent yet. I'll brief the team once local officers are on scene. But start digging. Every incident, every connection, everything tied to her name. I want it ready."

I hung up. The silence after felt louder than the call.

One more thing I needed to do, and I had to make it quick. No time to think, no time to hesitate.

Just move.

As I headed back toward Badwater Basin, the signal bars on my phone disappeared one by one.

Perfect.

I veered off the road and found a narrow trail that cut between two tall cliffs, the kind of place no one would stumble into by accident.

The silence out here was absolute—no wind, no hum of insects, just the faint tick of the engine cooling.

I popped the trunk. The metallic scent of blood hit me, crisp and dry.

Everything I couldn't risk keeping was inside: the sand soaked with Lucy's blood, Nick's clothes, the rags, the weapon, the gloves. Every trace of what happened. Every thread that could unravel it all.

Fires draw attention. Even out here. I checked the horizon—still dark, stars fading, a pale rim of light beginning to climb behind the mountains. I still had time before sunrise made the smoke visible.

I dragged out a small metal bin, filled it with everything, and drenched it in gasoline. The fumes burned my nose, caught in my throat. One spark from a match, and it all went up—an instant, hungry blaze that hissed and spat against the rock.

Seconds stretched into minutes. I stood there, jaw clenched, watching it all burn away—every lie, every mistake, every drop of blood.

When the flames finally weakened, I shoveled sand over them until nothing, but heat shimmered above the dirt. I buried the bin deep, tamped the ground flat until it looked untouched.

I poured a little water over the shovel, swirling it until the dirt loosened and slid away, then let it drip onto the gravel. Mud pooled at my feet, darkening the ground as the metal caught the light. Whatever marks had been there were gone—or smeared enough to be useless.

I slid it back into the trunk among the other tools, the shovel just another shape in the clutter. If anyone asked, I'd say it was my wife's. For the garden. Something ordinary. Something no one would look twice at.

By the time I drove off, the first light of dawn was spilling over the desert. The horizon burned gold, washing over the cliffs, the sand, the place I'd tried to erase. For a moment, it almost looked holy, like the world was pretending it hadn't seen what I'd done.

***

When I got back Nick was slumped against his car door, eyes hollow, hands still slick and dark. The wind moved around him, but he didn't seem to feel it. He looked up when he heard my boots crunch over the gravel.

"Is it done?" he asked. His voice cracked, thin and uneven, like something inside him had splintered and refused to mend.

"Yeah," I said quietly.

"It's done."

The words came out steady, but a cold weight pressed through me as I said them. It wasn't the truth. Not really. But Nick didn't need the truth right now, not when he was barely holding on.

He swallowed hard.

"She's gone?"

"She's gone," I told him. "And no one's going to find her."

Nick nodded slowly, then winced, like the words themselves hurt.

"What'd you tell them?"

"That she killed them both," I said. "Lilah and your dad. Then she ran off into the desert after. No car, no phone. They'll assume she's out on foot

somewhere, maybe hitched a ride or got hit by wild-
life. Happens out here all the time."

He didn't answer right away, just rubbed his
palms against his jeans. I watched him stand against
the hood, staring at the desert horizon like it held answers he didn't want to see. His hands twitched.

"Nick," I said, steady, "here's the thing—you
give them the details up until your dad. Just that.
Who was attacked first, what happened, everything
leading up to him." I let the words hang for a beat,
letting him imagine the sequence without panicking.

Then I leaned closer. "Then you say... she saw
me, got scared, and ran for it. That's it. Nothing else.
No guessing, no filling gaps. Just the facts."

He blinked, swallowed hard. "And if they ask...
why didn't anyone stop her?"

"You weren't in a position to," I said. "You did
what you could. Tell them I tried to, but it was too
dark to see anything. Keep your voice calm. Even if
it shakes, even if your chest feels like it's going to
split, just answer and move on. Don't add, don't explain."

He nodded, trying to force it, and I could see the
tension in his shoulders loosen slightly.

"Okay," he whispered.

"Good," I said, pressing a hand to his shoulder.

"Focus on the facts. That's all they need. I'll manage the rest."

"Adam…" he started, but his voice trailed off.

"Hey." I crouched down next to him. "You stick to the story. Don't add to it. Don't try to fix it. When they question you, you say what we rehearsed and nothing else."

Nick finally nodded. His face was pale, unreadable. "What about you?" he asked quietly.

"I got it, don't worry about me," I said. "Once they're done questioning us—assuming they don't hold us for too long, they'll probably make us stay in town. We'll get a motel, clean up. It sounds simple, but we need to be ready for it. Mentally."

The silence that followed was heavy. The air still carried the metallic tang of blood drying into the sand.

Nick finally exhaled.

"You think she deserved it?"

"Don't," I said, my voice harsher than I meant. I looked past him toward the horizon instead.

The wind picked up as the sun was rising, washing the desert in red and gold, scouring the ground clean. Long shadows stretched across the cracked ground as faint flashes of red and blue began to blink in the distance.

I set a hand on his shoulder. "We wait here. Answer what we need to. After that... we get out of this place, clean up, and figure out what comes next."

***

We didn't have long to sit in the silence before the first cruiser appeared on the horizon. The desert swallowed sound until the sirens were almost on top of us—lights flashing across the salt flats like lightning.

Two uniformed deputies stepped out, followed by a detective I didn't recognize. Morning light flashed off their sunglasses.

"You the ones who called it in?"

"I am," I said, flashing my badge. "Detective Adam Chaplin. Out of state."

I nodded toward Nick.

"I was tracking a suspect connected to an ongoing case—author C. Holloway. Things got out of control."

That got their attention.

I caught Nick glancing up at me from the corner of my eye as soon as I mentioned the case. I met his gaze briefly and gave a subtle look—it's okay.

The detective's expression sharpened. "C. Holloway? You're telling me he is a she and she's involved in this?"

"She is," I said. "She's the suspect. Still at large. Nick was targeted by her; he was in danger."

They separated us fast—standard procedure.

Nick looked dazed, barely standing, and I didn't blame him. The deserts sun was creeping higher, empty light that made it all feel unreal.

I was led to some chairs already set in place near one of the cruisers. The detective flashed me his badge that read Smith—funny coincidence, but I don't think he was in the mood to find it funny. He looked tired, the kind of tired that sits in your bones.

"Detective Chaplin, I'm Detective Shane Smith," he said, flipping open a small notepad. The paper edges were curled from the heat, his handwriting a tight scrawl I could barely make out. "You want to tell me what the hell happened out here?"

The crime scene looked almost serene in the light, like the desert was trying to bleach it clean.

"Yeah," I said, forcing my voice to stay even. "I was tracking an active suspect Lucy Rivers, also known as C. Holloway. She's linked to open cases back in Edenridge. I had reason to believe she fled this way."

I pulled her phone from my pocket. "I took this while she was detained."

Smith held out a hand, and I placed the phone in his palm. He tucked it into his pocket for later, pen scratching steadily across the page. I could hear the soft hum of radios in the background and the occasional snap of a camera shutter.

"And the other man—Nicholas Smith. You two know each other?"

I tried to defuse the tension, even if it was the wrong time for it. "Do you?" I said, half a smile tugging at my mouth.

He didn't flinch. Just stared. The desert light caught the hard line of his jaw.

I cleared my throat, the joke dying before it even landed. "Yeah," I said quietly. "We do."

"How long?"

"Since high school," I said, eyes drifting toward Nick in the distance—near another cruiser, head bowed, a paramedic crouched beside him. "He's an old friend."

Smith jotted that down, but his expression didn't change. The kind of look that said he already didn't like what that meant. I felt the sweat gathering at my collar, the grit of sand on my tongue.

Smith looked up at me, eyes narrowing just slightly. "That's not nothing. So, this wasn't just a random civilian?"

"No," I admitted. "He's been in contact with me about a cold case involving his ex-fiancée. I thought he might be in danger. She was escalating."

He leaned back, pen tapping against his notebook.

"So, you were personally involved with someone connected to a homicide investigation that was assigned to you?"

"He wasn't connected to the crimes," I said—quicker than I meant to.

His pen froze mid-scratch. I forced a breath through my nose, steadied my tone.

"He was a target. Lucy was using his life as a template for her books. She fixated on him."

Smith's brow furrowed. "Fixated how?"

I rubbed a hand over my face, desert dust sticking to my skin. "Characters, settings, dialogue—all pointed towards him. Her books read like she was documenting his life in real time." My throat felt dry, "When I connected that, I knew this wasn't just fiction anymore."

Smith leaned in a little, eyes sharp. "And you can prove that?"

"Yeah," I said, quieter now.

"A journal I found at the lake house back home—it had details in it, things about the cases no one else could have known unless they were there." I hesitated, biting back the words. "It wasn't fiction anymore. It was fixation, escalating into something else."

Smith let that hang for a moment.

The wind picked up, carrying the smell of dust and blood. I felt it cling to my clothes.

"Before she fled the scene, when did you last have contact with Lucy?" he asked.

"On the road," I said. "She was in cuffs."

I drew a breath. "She tried to attack me at the lake house before we left. Nick's father was there too."

Smith's pen scratched across the page, steady, methodical.

"During transport, I had her write a statement," I continued. "I know it's not standard procedure, but it was the only way I could keep things under control."

I met his eyes. "Her handwriting matched the journal I mentioned earlier. Same slant. Same spacing. That's when I confirmed she was Holloway."

He jotted a few more notes, eyes flicking between me and the stretch of desert behind, an endless canvas of dust and shadow. The wind carried the faint smell of smoke, or maybe memory.

"And after that?" he asked.

"She escaped," I said, my throat tightening.

"Since he didn't have his phone on him, I tried to get to Nick before she did."

He looked up, steadily. "And when did the attack happen?"

"Between one-thirty and two last night."

My voice faltered, the words dragging against the dry air. "By the time I got there, one victim was already down."

His pen paused. "Who?"

"I didn't know her personally. Never seen her before. But... I think she was Nick's friend, he said her name was Lilah."

Smith keeps writing. "And the second victim?"

I swallowed hard, words sticking in my mouth.

"His father... he came with me, but he got out of the car fast. Unfortunately, he got in between Lucy and Nick, I didn't have the chance to stop him."

For a long moment, neither of us spoke. Smith exhaled, low and almost like a prayer. "Jesus."

A pause sits between us.

"And you said she fled on foot?" he pressed, eyes narrowing toward the scene as the wind swept sand across the ground.

"She saw me, panicked, and ran. Headed east. I tried to follow, but it was pitch-dark out here. She left the road and disappeared into the landscape." I kept my tone even, careful not to give him anything beyond what I'd planned.

Detective Smith leaned back. "Too bad you didn't have all your gear with you. Taser, maybe... something?"

"I left the taser in my console," I said, keeping my tone measured. "I had the flashlight, but she'd already gotten a head start—at least two hundred feet across the flats. I could see her moving, but not well enough to take a shot safely. Firing blindly would've been wasted bullets... maybe worse."

Smith raised an eyebrow. "She took off out here? In Death Valley? Hopefully, she hitched a ride... or just got lucky with the terrain. But there are mountain lions out here..." His voice carried a teasing lilt, but it didn't land that way.

What the hell?

Is he trying to get in my head?

"Yeah, that's real comforting to know," I muttered, glancing at the desert. "I considered chasing," I continued, "but the distance and darkness made it reckless. Better to track and wait for the next move than make a mistake I couldn't take back."

He scribbled for a moment, eyes narrowing.

"Any other witnesses? Anyone who might've seen what happened?"

I shook my head, keeping my voice steady though my stomach twisted. "Other than Nick, not really. Out here… it's the middle of nowhere. Maybe one or two cars passed, but they didn't stop."

Smith's pen hovered over his notebook.

"So… basically a ghost town. Perfect crime scene." His tone was flat, almost sardonic.

"Exactly," I said, squinting against the glare of the rising sun. "Just the wind, the sand… and what had already happened."

He scribbled notes with calm precision. Then he looked up, voice cutting through the desert hush.

"And you didn't call it in sooner?"

I clenched my jaw, feeling the desert heat crawl into my nerves. "I tried. Out here… nothing. No bars, no signal. Had to drive out to reach a line."

He flipped to a new page, "And why were you alone on this? Don't you usually have a partner? Where was Nick when you made the call?"

"Here," I said, glancing toward the distant horizon, "I made him stay put. Didn't want anyone tampering with the scene. And I do have a partner… but this wasn't official. The case was cold—personal at that point."

"Personal," he repeated, voice flat, with a hint of mock admiration, like he was reading the most cli- chéd line in a police movie.

"Yeah," I muttered.

"Personal."

He studied me for a moment longer, then leaned forward, elbows on his knees, "I've got a feeling you're leaving something out."

I met his gaze.

"It's a crazy and messed-up story. Lucy is psy- chotic. You'll read it in my report."

Smith's expression didn't change.

"You understand how this looks, right? You drive across state lines with a suspect, looking for a friend who might be in danger. Then you chase her after finding out she's tied to multiple homicides— with that friend at risk. And you end up at a double scene before the local PD even gets the call."

"Yeah," I said. "I understand."

"Okay, just making sure," he said in another teasing tone, making him a bit harder to read. He didn't say anything else right away. I could feel the judgment under his calm, the unspoken suspicion— the kind I'd had to wear before.

A few seconds passed, then he spoke again.

"You know how this goes, right? We're going to need Nick's clothes. Send it in for evidence—blood on it. You won't get your vehicles back for a while; we need to inspect them."

I nodded. "Understood. How long you think that'll take?"

He shrugged slightly. "Depends. Could be a few days for the lab to process, depending on the workload. The vehicles? They could be held for several hours to a day. Standard procedure—chain of custody, fingerprinting, anything left at the scene. You already know, nothing you can rush."

After a beat, he stood.

"You'll give a full written statement before leaving town. Don't go without clearance from the local PD."

"Understood."

He paused, then glanced toward where Nick sat near a cruiser, head lowered, eyes distant. "For what it's worth, you look like hell, Detective."

"Yeah," I said, rubbing a hand over my face, "feels about right."

Another uniformed man approached, squinting against the harsh morning light bouncing off the salt flats. He looked at me, then glanced toward Nick, who sat slumped against the hood of a patrol SUV, hands trembling, face pale.

"Detective Chaplin?" the officer said, voice hesitant. "We're having trouble getting anything coherent out of—"

I cut him off, low but firm.

"He just witnessed two people close to him get murdered—stabbed—by someone he considered a childhood friend. Cut him some slack."

The officer froze, blinking as the wind stirred sand around our boots. "Right... I—"

"Right," I said, letting my gaze sweep over the empty basin, the distant cliffs, the bloodstains fading in the sun. "He's not a suspect. He's a witness. He's in shock. Give him time. You'll get your statements when he can talk without shaking apart."

I glanced at Nick. His jaw was stiff, eyes fixed on the cracked ground, hands clenching and unclenching. He flinched at every distant sound, every shifting shadow.

I placed a hand lightly on his shoulder.

"Take it slow with him. He's still here, still processing. You'll get what you need."

Nick's hands shook as he gripped the edge of the chair. "I... I was with Lilah. We were just talking, and..." His voice broke, trailing off.

289

I was pulled off to the side to let Nick speak, standard procedure, but I could still see him, hear him and he could see me.

Detective Smith sat down in the chair across from him and leaned forward. "Take your time, Nick. Just breathe."

Nick swallowed, eyes darting briefly to me, then back to the ground. "And... out of nowhere... Lucy... she just..." He pressed his palms to his face.

"She took her life."

Smith's pen hovered over his notepad. "Okay... go on. What happened next?"

He drew in a shaky breath. "My dad... he tried to help... but... Lucy... she... took his life too."

I stayed silent, watching him. No one could untangle this for him.

No Clay.

Just Nick.

Nick's eyes flicked toward me, searching, then away. "As soon as she saw Adam... she ran."

Smith nodded, writing something down. "She ran when Adam arrived?"

"Yeah... he... he ran after her, but..." His voice cracked again. "It was dark. Too dark to see... she ran off. East. I think east."

I gave him a subtle nod, letting him know he was doing okay, that he could keep going.

"Eastbound into the desert?" Smith asked softly.

"Yeah... I think," Nick whispered. His shoulders trembled. "I don't know... I couldn't... I just..."

Smith tries reassuring Nick, "It's okay. Just keep talking."

Nick exhaled shakily, then began again, haltingly, reconstructing the rest of the night piece by piece, each word a struggle but eventually forming a full, if raw, account.

Detective Smith walked up to me, expression calm but firm. "We're going to need to hold your vehicles for now," he said. "You're not suspects, but you were the last to see her—the only ones. We just need to clear a few things."

I nodded, "Understood."

One of the local officers gestured toward a cruiser, "We'll drive you to a motel nearby while the cars are processed. But first, we need to handle things here."

Nick stood stiffly, shoulders tense. An officer knelt beside him. "Nick, before you change, we need to take some quick swabs from your hands and arms. Standard procedure."

Nick froze, voice trembling. "Sw... swabs?"

"Just a few samples of any visible blood," the officer said gently. "It won't hurt. Then you can change into clean clothes."

I stepped closer, voice low. "It's okay, Nick. Just a few seconds."

He nodded shakily and held his hands out. The officer swabbed his palms and forearms methodically. Nick's face was tense, shoulders rigid, but he let them work.

"Done," the officer said after a moment. "You're clear to change now."

Behind a temporary privacy screen, Nick swapped into clean clothes the officers had provided. His blood-stained shirt and pants were carefully bagged as evidence, and the RV was checked for fingerprints and other traces of information. Nick kept his hands fidgeting at his sides, distant and pale, but at least he was no longer wearing the bloodied clothes.

Meanwhile, I pulled my bag and phone from my car. Detective Smith came up, expression neutral.

"Adam," he said, "standard procedure: a quick look through your bag."

I handed it over. He rifled through it carefully, eyes lingering briefly on my phone. "You can keep this but keep it off and don't contact anyone about the case."

"Got it," I said.

Smith zipped the bag closed and nodded toward Nick. "We've cleared what he's taking, too. Anything personal that isn't contaminated—you can keep."

Nick's fingers hovered over a clean pair of socks he was allowed to keep. A small relief, but his shoulders remained tight.

Once everything was cleared, the officers ushered us to the cruiser. The ride to the motel was quiet, the desert stretching endlessly on either side. Nick slumped into the back seat, hands in his lap, eyes hollow. I stayed quiet beside him, letting him just breathe, just exist without interference.

Miles later, we arrived at a motel, the kind that hadn't been remodeled since the '70s. Nick collapsed onto the bed, eyes empty. I shut the door behind us and finally let my breath go.

My breath stifled in my lungs, my mind already running through the next steps. Now it was just Nick and me, waiting for the storm to hit, for the officers to come knocking.

I glanced over at him, saw the strain in his shoulders, the way he kept rubbing at his temples. We had to get our story straight—every word, every hesitation accounted for. One slip, one wrong move, and all of this would come crashing down.

I reached into my bag, fingers grazing the worn leather until they closed around what I needed. The stack of papers was heavier than I expected, the edges slightly curled, but orderly copies of Lucy's journal, printed from the photos I'd taken back at the lake house.

I laid them out on the motel desk with deliberate care, letting the faint fluorescent light catch the pages. Each one felt like a quiet echo of everything we'd been through.

"Before we do anything else, you need to see this," I said, keeping my voice low, measured. Nick leaned over, hesitant, eyes dark and wary as they scanned the first page. The desert sun had left him drained, and even here he looked fragile, like a candle flickering against a draft.

"I only read the most recent entries at your lake house," I continued, my thumb brushing over a line without really touching the words. "I didn't realize it was Lucy. Even when I printed these off, I barely had time to glance at them. Your dad read a little to me on the way up here… but it's different seeing it yourself."

He reached for a page but paused, as if the act of touching the ink might pull him into it. I could feel the tension coiling in the small space between us, thick and almost suffocating.

I could see it in his posture, in the way he lingered over certain words in the journal: recognition, disbelief, a quiet fury. We had talked it through. We'd faced parts of it together.

I cleared my throat.

"And... one more thing. I didn't tell you everything last night."

His head snapped up, eyes narrowing.

"Lucy..." I swallowed, trying to keep my voice steady.

"She's not buried. I didn't do it."

A long pause.

I could almost feel the weight of that confession pressing against the thin motel walls.

"I let... nature take care of her,"

I said, choosing my words carefully.

"There was a mountain lion. That's how it happened."

Nick's face went pale, and for a moment, I wondered if I'd said more than he could manage. But he said nothing, just turned back to the pages, letting the journal do the rest of the work.

By morning, we'd have to face the world outside this motel, the cops, the questions. But for now, this was the calm before it all. Pages on a desk, two men holding pieces of a story that no one else could ever fully understand.

ten

The smell of summer pavement. The sound of cicadas. Lucy's small hand wrapped around mine.

Before.

I met Lucy before I even knew what friendship was supposed to mean.

Preschool—naptime and juice boxes. She had this wild, crooked smile that made you feel like you were already in trouble just for standing next to her.

My mom used to say Lucy was "a little intense." I thought that meant she just cared a lot.

Back then, my mom was different. Softer. She laughed more. She loved me, she loved my dad, and for a while, everything felt simple. We went to church every Sunday. Sometimes, Lucy came with us.

I was a restless kid during mass, one of those who couldn't sit still or stay quiet for long. Maybe I was bored. Maybe I just wanted attention. Or maybe

I wanted to make Lucy laugh. Either way, I was tough to manage.

Whenever I lost my temper—broke something, yelled, cried—Lucy would grab my hand and whisper, "It's not your fault. That wasn't you. It was Clay."

I didn't know who Clay was. I thought maybe she made him up, like kids do. But I liked the idea that there was someone else to blame.

Lucy and I didn't really have other friends. We didn't need them—or at least, that's what she told me. It was always just us. She said no one else would ever understand the way we did. And maybe she was right, because the more time I spent with her, the less I wanted to be around anyone else.

We were inseparable. Years blurred together, scraped knees, whispered secrets, and that quiet certainty that Lucy and I were different from everyone else.

***

By the time we hit second or third grade, Clay wasn't just a name anymore.

He became real to me.

Easier to use.

The first time I blamed him aloud was when I brought a BB gun to school.

Some kid laughed at me, so I shot him in the foot.

I don't even remember pulling the trigger.

Just the sound—a pop, the boy screaming, the look on everyone's faces. My stomach turned to ice. And then Lucy was there, grabbing my wrist, her voice calm and sure.

"It was you, wasn't it, Clay?"

When the police officers showed up, I panicked. My mom and dad were furious, the kind of furious that made the air go still. My mom's voice cracked when she yelled, and my dad looked like he wanted to shoot me with the same BB gun.

"Who's Clay?" my mom asked, gripping my shoulders so stiff I couldn't look away.

"Lucy told me that every time I get mad or do something bad, it's Clay's fault, not mine," I said. My voice was small. I was only nine.

She just stared at me for a long time. Her eyes shifted—confusion, fear, something else. I thought she might cry. Instead, she said quietly, "Lucy's not coming over anymore."

I'm only finding out now that Lucy wrote about that day in her journal.

10/14/2004 — Nick's mom is mean. She doesn't like me. She said I'm bad for Nick, but she's the bad one. She makes him sad. My mom and dad said I can't go to school with Nick anymore. They said I need to stay home. That's so stupid. Nick needs me. We're supposed to be together forever. He said he'll miss me, but I know he'll still think about me. He always does. One day, we'll live together, and his mom won't be there to stop us.

Even now, reading it makes my skin crawl.

I remember the note she left outside my window, tucked into our hiding spot—our secret place. The handwriting was messy, rushed: "Meet me at the base this weekend. Just us."

And I went.

Of course I went. I was nine, and she was my best friend. I was happy she still wanted to see me after everything, the police, my parents, the BB gun. She was the only one who understood Clay. So, I kept sneaking out. I'd tell my parents I was at another friend's house, and they believed me.

Eventually, I started making new friends at school, but no one ever came close to Lucy. No one ever would, not till Adam. No matter how much time passed, Lucy was always there.

***

Seven months after the BB gun incident, after turning ten, I broke a picture frame in the living room.

It was one of my parents' wedding photos, the one where my mom's hair was still long and my dad actually smiled. I didn't even remember throwing it. I just remembered the sound—glass shattering, my mom screaming my name.

"Nick!" she shouted, rushing over. "What is wrong with you lately?"

I blinked at the floor, my ears ringing.

"I didn't do it," I said quietly.

Her voice cracked, "Then who did?"

"Clay."

Her hands went to her face like she was trying not to cry or scream. "You have to stop blaming this imaginary person every time you mess up."

"I'm not lying!" I yelled, my pulse racing. "He gets mad, not me!"

"Enough!" she snapped. "You have to take re-sponsibility—"

I didn't remember what happened next. One second, she was talking, the next I was on the floor, kicking, screaming, pounding my fists onto the carpet so hard it burned my skin. The words coming out of my mouth didn't even sound like me. My voice slightly dropped, rough, angry.

"I said it wasn't me!"

My dad grabbed my arms and pulled me up.

"Nick! That's enough!"

His voice was shaking. "Honey, go sit down, you shouldn't get worked up like this."

My mom stood frozen, staring at me like I wasn't her son anymore, pale, her hand resting over her stomach.

"I'm fine," she said, though her voice was trembling. "Are you sure we're going to be ready for this baby?"

My dad sighed, rubbing the back of his neck.

"You're overthinking it. It's just the mood swings."

When it was over, I broke down crying. I told them both I was sorry, repeatedly, clinging to my dad like I was afraid he'd disappear. My hands were raw and bleeding from the carpet burns.

He let out another sigh and said softly, almost to himself, "He's just acting out. It's probably a phase."

But my mom didn't say anything. She just picked up the broken frame, her hands trembling, and whispered, "You don't understand. I saw his eyes. That wasn't Nick."

His voice was calm in the way that made it worse, "Honey, he's a kid. He's got an active imagination."

She turned to him, eyes red, "He's brought a BB gun to school. That's not imagination."

They started whisper-fighting—like they always did when they didn't want me to hear.

But I heard everything.

Mom thought something was wrong with me.

Dad thought I'd grow out of it.

And all I could think was—if Clay's not real, then why don't I remember doing it?

I kept blaming Clay for everything bad that happened. Every fight, every tantrum—it was easier that way.

Eventually, Mom stopped trying to correct me. I was hardly ever home to cause trouble anymore. My parents were too busy working, saving, and planning for a bigger family.

And me? I was too caught up in Lucy. In our secret world where everything made sense.

***

The day I told her I was going to be a big brother, she leaned in close and whispered, "She doesn't love you anymore, Nick. That's why they're having another baby. To replace you. And guess what? I would never replace you."

I didn't believe her. Not at first. But as my mom's moods changed—the snapping, the silence, the way she seemed tired of me—Lucy's words stopped sounding crazy. They started sounding true.

***

My parents caught me sneaking out again, my mom gave in, she was seven months pregnant and didn't have the energy.

She said if I wanted to see Lucy, it had to be at our house. No more going out. No more secrets. I remember feeling a mix of relief and excitement—relief that I could still see her, and excitement that our world was still ours, even if it had to be hidden in plain sight.

Reading her journal, I couldn't help but shiver. Even then, she was relentless, always finding a way back in. I flipped the page to an entry from that winter:

11/03/2005 — Yay! Nick's mom finally said I can come over again. I missed him so much! I'm gonna make sure she never tries to keep us apart again. I'm going to Nick's house today! We'll play all our games and maybe make up new ones. Nothing can stop us!

Nick and I are meant to be together forever. He just doesn't know it yet.

A month later, it was clear she was already frustrated with the "obstacle" in our way:

12/12/2005 — Nick's mom still doesn't like me, even though she lets me come over now. She kept watching us the whole time, even when we were just playing. It's not my fault she got in the way.

I didn't realize then how far that little seed of anger would grow... until that afternoon at the top of the stairs.

We were fueled by candy. Playing when my mom rounded the corner with wrapped presents stacked in her hands, her voice was sharp and tired.

"Slow down!"

Lucy laughed—a wild, fearless laugh, and started running circles around her.

I tried to grab Lucy, to pull her back, but she spun faster, a whirlwind I couldn't stop, until—

I can still see it.

The way my mom's hands flailed in the air before she fell.

The sound her body made when it hit the bottom.

That's when she miscarried.

Everyone said it was an accident.

Kids being kids.

But my mom never believed that.

She swore one of us pushed her. And when she looked at me, I couldn't meet her eyes.

***

After my mom's miscarriage, everything changed.

She'd stop in the middle of a sentence sometimes and stare off, like she was watching ghosts walk by. The bottles started showing up after that. And when she drank, she saw the worst parts of me— or maybe she just needed somewhere to put her pain.

She talked less, yelled more. Told me I couldn't see Lucy ever again. Said Lucy wasn't right. Said she brought something dark with her every time she was around.

Lucy always found her way back. I'd sneak out, lie or not, and they barely asked anymore.

I remember one night after the miscarriage. The house smelled like wine and burnt toast. Mom was sitting at the kitchen table, staring at nothing.

"Why do you always break everything you touch?" she said. Her voice was low, flat.

"I didn't mean to."

She laughed—a sound that didn't sound like her anymore.

"You never mean to. You just do."

I wanted to tell her it wasn't me, that it was Clay again. But I'd stopped saying his name around her.

Dad came in a few minutes later, said nothing. Just picked up the empty glass and set it in the sink.

Nobody said goodnight.

***

It was almost a year after the fall when things got bad enough that I stopped recognizing home. The air always smelled like bleach and wine. Mom cleaned when she was angry.

She was angry a lot.

"Did you take money from my purse again?" she asked one night.

I hadn't. At least I didn't think I had.

"No," I said quietly.

She slammed the drawer shut.

"Don't lie to me, Nick. You've always been good at that."

"I'm not lying," I whispered, looking away…

"Then where the hell is it?"

I didn't have an answer. Sometimes things just went missing. Sometimes I found them later and didn't remember moving them.

When I didn't answer, she grabbed my arm—not hard, but enough to send a shiver through me.

"Look at me."

I did.

Her eyes were glassy, wet, full of something between hate and heartbreak.

"I wish you'd just tell me the truth," she said.

"I don't even know who you are anymore."

I almost said, me neither.

But instead, I just whispered, "I'm sorry," and went to my room.

Lucy was waiting by my window that night. She said, "She's never going to love you the way I do."

Back then, I thought she meant she cared. I didn't realize she meant something else entirely.

Lucy said she was protecting me from my mom. From the yelling, the bruises, the things I didn't want to admit were real. She was the only one who made me feel safe.

My dad never tried to protect me; he was always working, always finding excuses to stay away from mom. His version of help was keeping the Sunday routine alive, even after my mom stopped going— dragging me to church and telling me to pray, like that could fix everything.

Lucy told me he was angry with me too. Said if he really loved me, he would've left my mom and taken me with him. "But he didn't," she whispered, "so it's not you, Nick. It's them."

As I thought back to that day at the top of the stairs, something twists inside me—a slow, bitter churn I can't shake. My jaw tightens until I realize I'm grinding my teeth.

How could Lucy have done that? How did I ever believe she was innocent? I should've seen through her. She'd been manipulating me all along.

The thought of it ignited something hot in my chest. Anger, maybe, no—disgust. But then it shifted.

My mind flashed to what I did to her at Badwater Basin, and for a moment I was waiting for the guilt to hit me.

It didn't.

Instead, all I felt was... nothing. And that's what scared me most.

***

By the time we were twelve, my parents had finally had enough. They started locking the doors at night, making rules I couldn't wriggle around.

No more Lucy.

No more excuses.

If I wanted to see anyone, they had to come to our house. Back then I thought they were punishing me—locking me in with the yelling and the bruises. I hated them for it.

Now I can see they were trying to save me. They didn't know how to do it right, but they were trying.

Lucy didn't take it like that.

She hated being shut out.

08/20/2007 — My parents are sending me away. I heard them talking to Nick's parents through the door. His mom said I'm 'obsessed' with him and that I need serious help. That's not true. They just don't understand us.

Nick and I have been together since forever, he needs me. He just forgets sometimes.

They think keeping us apart will make him better, but it won't. He gets angry without me there. He doesn't know how to handle Clay yet. His mom doesn't see it, how she makes him that way. I see it. I always have.

I'll write to him every day if I need to. Maybe I'll sneak out before they take me. Nick would never let them take me away for good. He promised he wouldn't.

That night, my mom didn't wake up.

They investigated, and my dad took the fall— thinking it was me who killed her while he was at work. No one ever suspected Lucy. But reading this now, decades later, she wrote about that night like it was inevitable. Like my mom had to die for me to be free.

Lucy's parents sent her away after my mom's death—they didn't mention where, just that she needed better guidance.

I remembered the letters she sent me while she was gone. She wanted to make sure we never drifted apart. Wanted to remind me she was still there, still watching, still mine.

And I always wrote back.

I don't have those letters from her anymore. I got rid of them when I moved.

All except the first one.

That one, I couldn't throw away. Back then, it was the only thing that made me feel like someone still cared about me.

Dear Nick,

I'm really sorry about what happened to your mom. I heard about it, and it's hard to believe your dad would do that to her.

You know I'm here for you, right? I always will be. And so will Clay. Don't be scared of him, okay? He only comes out when you need him. He helps you. He takes away the bad feelings, so you don't have to feel them anymore.

I wish I could be there to make you feel better. I hate it here. The people talk too much, and nobody understands me like you do.

But don't worry, I'll get out soon. Then we can be together again, and nobody will stop us this time.

Love, Lucy.

Her handwriting was shaky but neat, like she was trying to look grown up. I kept that letter for years, still hidden under my bed. Even now, I can still picture those hearts bleeding purple ink into the paper.

***

Middle school was worse.

The whispers followed me everywhere—that's the kid whose mom died, the one whose dad is in prison. Teachers looked at me like I was a ticking bomb, waiting for a reason to explode.

And I did. More than once.

Foster homes never lasted. I'd lose my temper, break something, punch a wall and then pack my bags again. They said I was "angry," "damaged," "unsavable." Maybe they were right.

I never told anyone about Clay again, but I still blamed him. Quietly. Inside. Whenever I blacked out or lost control, it was easier to tell myself it wasn't me—that I hadn't even been there.

By high school, I stopped expecting people to stick around. I was used to being alone. They had me seeing a therapist for my anger issues. She told me to write out my feelings—one of the few suggestions I actually tried.

Whenever I wrote letters to Lucy, I felt calm, so maybe it made sense that writing worked. Funny, because now I'm an author—but back then, I hated school, hated books.

I wasn't some quiet kid lost in stories. I was broken, restless. The only time I felt steady was when I put words down or played baseball. Sometimes it was poems, sometimes short stories or lyrics—pieces of me I didn't know how else to say.

Then I met Adam.

***

We met in detention—me for mouthing off to a teacher, him for being late to class. He cracked a joke about teachers giving kids detention just so they wouldn't have to eat lunch alone. And for the first time in years, I laughed. It wasn't much, but it was enough.

After that, Adam and I started hanging out more. Being around him was different than being around Lucy. With Lucy, I always felt like I had to keep up—like she was pulling the strings. But with Adam, I could just be. He wasn't bossy and didn't need to fix me.

Lucy had been gone for a while, and life without her was... quieter, though not simple. I'd learned to rely on myself more. I was guarded and careful, but I was starting to make choices that were mine alone. Even though Clay showed up less often. He would usually show up in moments of frustration or when I felt trapped. I knew I had the final say.

I was denying his existence.

I was more independent, but I hadn't lost my old spark. If anything, I'd turned it into a shield. I liked making people laugh, testing boundaries, seeing how far I could push a joke before a teacher yelled at me.

I was the class clown, the one who made everyone groan or chuckle during class, who blurred the lines between harmless mischief and minor chaos. It was a way to feel alive; to prove I could still control something—my life.

I started choosing my own friends, spending afternoons at the library writing when I wanted to think instead of scheming, or on the baseball team, pushing my body in ways that felt good and controlled.

Yet even in those moments, Clay whispered, small and insistent, reminding me of everything I'd learned the hard way.

This was my life now.

My choices.

Somehow, Clay showed up less when Adam was around. And on the nights, he did, Adam always seemed to know how to bring me back, even though I never told him about Clay.

We were at this high school party after homecoming—red solo cups, bad music, the kind of night that smells like cheap beer and regret.

I drank too much and heard people whispering about me and Lucy. How she ditched me. How I was the "crazy foster kid." They didn't know anything— that we still wrote to each other, that she still cared.

Something inside me snapped that night.

It was Clay.

I don't remember everything after that—just Adam's voice cutting through the noise, yelling my name, his hand gripping my shoulder hard enough to keep me from breaking.

When I came to, he just looked at me and said, "You good, man?"

I wasn't. But I nodded anyway.

Lost in memory the TV hummed low across the motel room, washing the walls in a soft blue light. Adam's sitting at the foot of his bed, flipping through channels, half-focused. It's late—too late to still be awake, too early to go to sleep but neither of us could even think about sleep.

"You're doing that thing again," he says, eyes still on the screen.

"What thing?" I blinked, snapping out of my thoughts.

He glanced over. "That thing where your head goes somewhere else. You get this look—like you're trying to solve the whole damn world in your head."

I let out a small laugh, "Guess I'm predictable."

Adam smirked faintly, "Nah. Just loud, even when you're quiet."

The air felt heavy, not uncomfortable, just full.

"Do you ever think about that night?" I asked.

He raised an eyebrow. "Which one?"

"The party. Homecoming."

That got his attention. The remote stilled in his hand. He didn't look at me right away. "You mean when you almost got yourself killed for being an idiot?"

"Yeah," I murmur, eyes on the floor. "That one."

Adam leaned back against the headboard, sighing through his nose. "I remember you scaring the hell out of everyone. Thought you were going to kill that guy."

"I almost did."

"You got him good, though."

Adam studied me for a beat, his expression softening. "Whatever it was, you've come a long way since then."

I wish I believed him.

"That wasn't me, though," I said quietly.

He turned to me, his voice steady.

"I know."

There was a pause, long enough for the next commercial break to start.

"I put the pieces together," he added finally, his tone lower. "After Clay introduced himself to me."

My head snapped up. His eyes met mine, calm but knowing.

I didn't think anyone had ever noticed.

"You knew?" I asked, voice barely above a whisper.

Adam nodded once, "Yeah. I just didn't think you were ready to hear it."

The motel room smelled like damp carpet and old cigarettes. The kind of place meant for people passing through, not people hiding. Light from the TV pulsed against the faded wallpaper, painting Adam's face in ghostly blue.

He finally spoke. "They're going to keep digging, you know. The cops."

I didn't look up.

"You think I don't know that?"

He shrugged, the movement stiff.

"They're watching your house. Probably already tapped your phone. They'll want to see if Lucy reaches out—since they think she's still alive."

Alive.

That word hit harder than it should've.

I swallowed, my throat dry.

"And if they see she doesn't?"

"Then they'll start asking better questions," Adam said quietly. "Ones you can't afford to answer."

I leaned forward, pressing my palms against my face. "You think I don't replay it every second? What I did?"

Adam didn't answer. A low buzz filled the room—an old sitcom laugh track echoing off the walls like a mockery.

"You didn't do it alone," he said finally.

I looked up, "You shouldn't have helped me."

He held my stare, "You think I could've left you there? Covered in blood? Losing your mind?"

The silence that followed was heavier than the air itself.

"They'll find her," I said quietly.

"Not with what happened," Adam replied flatly.

The air seemed too thin.

"You shouldn't say that." I murmured.

He gave a dry, hollow laugh.

"You shouldn't have done it."

That one cut deep. I looked away.

After another long pause, Adam rubbed his face, his voice tired. "Look. We stick to the story. Lucy's gone. Missing. You don't know where she went. That's it."

I nodded slowly.

"I know you don't have your phone on you but be careful," he added. "They'll watch your texts, your calls. And when they can't find a body, they'll circle back to you."

"Then what?" I asked.

He stared at the TV screen.

"If we stick to the story, they'll eventually stop poking. If they happen to find something we missed, then we start running."

Static replaced the show, buzzing like white noise in my ears. My reflection stared back at me in the dark glass—eyes hollow, jaw clenched. For a split second, there she was behind me.

Lucy.

Smiling.

I blinked.

Gone.

I turned toward Adam. "Does it replay in your mind?"

Adam didn't look at me when he spoke.

"Every second," he said quietly. "So, say what you need to say, Nick. Because once we walk out that door, this conversation and the truth about last night, never happened. We don't talk about it to anyone. Not even each other."

His words lingered, heavy in the air. The motel TV flickered with muted light, shadows crawling up the walls.

Knowing what he just said, I knew I had to ask while I still could.

Time wasn't on our side.

***

"So… how did Lucy show up on her own?" I asked. "I figured you all would've come together. I understand now, why my dad put her in handcuffs before we took off."

Adam finally turned toward me, his face was pale under the dim yellow lamp. "It was a mess," he said, exhaling slowly. "Something about her was off from the start. After what she pulled at the lake house—trying to kill me and your dad—I'm lucky he cuffed her. If he hadn't…"

He shook his head.

"She would've finished the job."

He leaned back against the headboard, rubbing a hand over his face. "We were on the road for hours. Stopped at a rest area to sleep a bit. She asked to use the bathroom—at first, I made her go on the side of the road. Didn't trust her. I felt like an asshole, but I wasn't taking chances. She kept playing the innocent card. Said she just needed a minute. She'd been doing that the whole drive—pretending she was scared, sorry, whatever would work."

I stayed quiet, just listening.

"I made her fill out a quick statement for me," Adam went on, voice lower now. "Something to cover myself in case she ran. And when I saw her handwriting… It hit me. It matched the journal I found at the lake house. The one I thought was Clay's."

He met my eyes.

"I don't know why, but I never realized until then that Lucy and Clay were the same damn voice in your life."

Something inside me twisted.

"Before I knew it, she was gone," Adam said, his tone hollow. "I tried making it to Death Valley as fast as I could. I knew you'd be in trouble with her loose."

He paused, staring at the floor. "I'm sorry about your friend. And your dad. I should've stopped him before things went south."

"It's okay," I said quietly.

"Her time was almost up anyway. I don't know what condition she had, but… she told me she had less than a year left to live." I swallowed hard. "And my dad—" My voice broke a little. "I just wanted to tell him I'm sorry, for ever thinking he killed my mom."

Adam's expression softened. He reached out and set a hand on my shoulder. "You know he said the same thing about you," he said, "me and your dad talked quite a bit on the way up here. If you want to hear about it."

I nodded, eyes burning.

***

He gave a faint smile. "He told me about when you were a kid. Before everything went wrong. Said things used to be… peaceful—before your moms' miscarriage. He wished he'd done more for you. Said he'd give anything to go back."

The room went quiet again, the hum of the air conditioner filling the silence between us.

"He told me this story," he said. "About when you were maybe six or seven. You two were out by the lake near your old house. Said you brought him a bunch of rocks and told him you were 'building something that could last forever.'"

I frowned, trying to remember.

"He said you stacked them one by one, all crooked," Adam went on with a faint smile, "but you wouldn't stop until it looked right. He called it 'Nick's tower.'"

A quiet laugh escaped me, "It fell apart the next morning."

"Yeah," Adam said softly. "But he said you didn't cry. You just picked them up and started over. Told him, 'I'll just build it better this time.' He said he never forgot that."

The room felt still as the memory flashed through my mind, "He remembered that?"

"Every detail," Adam said. "Even the way the light hit the water that day. Your dad said it was the first time in a long time he'd felt proud."

I looked away, blinking fast.

"Guess I ruined that feeling later on."

Adam sighed.

"You didn't ruin anything. You both got lost in the same storm, that's all."

For a moment, neither of us said anything. The motel clock ticked faintly.

I stared at the dusty carpet, then whispered, "He didn't deserve what happened."

Adam nodded slowly, "No one did."

The silence stretched again, heavier this time—and for a moment, Lucy's shadow felt like it was standing right there between us.

I rubbed my hands together. "It's crazy," I said, barely audible. "Lucy used to tell me that too. About storms. How some of us are just meant to get caught in them."

Adam turned his head, "You thinking about her again?"

"Yeah," I admitted. "About that time on the football field."

Adam's eyes softened but he didn't speak. Just waited. And before I knew it, my mind drifted back to the night Lucy confessed, and everything that came before we both broke for good.

***

The field behind the school was quiet that afternoon. Just the hum of wind in the grass and the distant echo of the track team wrapping up practice. I was waiting for Adam—he was running late, like always—when I saw her.

Lucy.

She stood by the bleachers, sunlight catching on her hair. For a second, it almost felt like old times. Like everything that happened hadn't happened.

"Nick?" Her voice carried across the field, small but familiar.

"Lucy?" I blinked, not sure if I was seeing right. "You're back?"

She smiled—that soft, nostalgic kind of smile that didn't quite reach her eyes.

"Surprise."

Before I could react, she crossed the distance and threw her arms around me.

Her hug lingered. I tensed a little, caught off guard, but hugged her back anyway. When she finally pulled away, her gaze held mine longer than it should've.

Then she leaned in—quick, certain—going for a kiss.

I stepped back before she reached me. Her eyes widened. "What's wrong?" she asked, voice trembling just enough to sound wounded. "Aren't you happy to see me?"

"Well, yeah, of course I am," I said slowly, trying to ease the tension. "But—"

"But what?" she pressed. "Is there someone else?"

I shook my head, "No. I'm not dating anyone, Lucy. I just…"

The words stuck. How do you tell someone you care about them, just not the way they want?

She searched my face for an answer I didn't have.

The silence between us thickened.

Then, "Nick!"

Adam's voice broke the air like a snap of thunder.

We both turned as he jogged across the field toward us, waving. Lucy's entire posture shifted—shoulders tightening, expression guarded.

"Sorry I'm late," Adam said, glancing between us. "Didn't know you had company."

Lucy's smile returned, but it was paper thin, "I was just leaving."

I tried reaching for her.

"Lucy, wait—"

She was already walking away, brushing past Adam with a polite nod that didn't hide the sharpness in her tone. "Nice to meet you."

We stood there in the empty field, watching her go.

Adam gave a small whistle.

"So... that was Lucy?"

I exhaled; eyes still fixed on the spot where she'd been standing a second ago. The field faded, replaced by the dim yellow light of the motel room.

"That was Lucy."

I hadn't meant to say it aloud.

Adam's voice cut through the TV, low and steady, "I figured," he said, like he knew exactly which memory I was trapped in.

The memory faded, but the feeling didn't.

"I never told you this part, but she tried to kiss me," I said finally. "That day on the field, right before you showed up."

Adam looked up, startled, "Seriously?"

"Yeah. I didn't even know how to react. She wasn't like that before... Something was different. Off."

Adam exhaled slowly, "That was the first time I saw her. I remember thinking she looked... wired. Too calm for someone who just got back from wherever she went."

"She asked if there was someone else," I said. "I told her no. I saw her as family but maybe that was the wrong answer."

Adam frowned, "Nick, there was no right answer with Lucy. You know that now."

I nodded, though the guilt still stuck to me like smoke. "I just keep replaying that day. Maybe if I'd done something differently—"

He cut me off gently. "You didn't make her who she was, and everything that's happened... wasn't your fault."

I wished I could believe him.

***

I sat on the edge of the motel bed; the lettered pages of Lucy's journals spread in front of me like a trail of breadcrumbs I wasn't sure I wanted to follow.

Every page carried the smell of old ink, the obsessive scrawl of a girl who saw the world only in terms of me.

The entries shifted. Adam. My present-day Adam. The one who had always tried to keep me grounded, even before he knew what was real.

10/04/2014 — Adam was at school with Nick today. I don't like him. He's trying to take Nick away from me, even though he doesn't know it. Clay agrees, he doesn't trust Adam either. Nick looks at him like he's a friend, but I see through it. Adam laughs at Nick's jokes. Adam touches Nick's shoulder.

Adam thinks he can protect Nick. He can't. Not from me. Not from Clay. Not from what I know he needs.

I swallowed hard. Reading her thoughts about Adam made my skin crawl.

When Adam was around, Nick didn't notice the way I looked at him. I had to wait. Plan. I can't let Adam interfere. I can't let anyone interfere. Clay and I know what's best. I'll wait for the right moment. I'll make sure no one comes between us again.

I tossed the journal on the bed. The motel room was quiet except for the TV and the hum of the air conditioner. I could feel Adam's presence from where he was half-asleep on the bed, a mug of coffee in his hand.

03/21/2018 — Claire showed up at school today. I hate her. She smiles at him, laughs at his jokes, and I can't stand it. Nick is mine. She thinks she can take him away. Clay agrees, she doesn't understand what he needs. I will make sure she never gets close. Never. If she really loved Nick, she wouldn't exist in his life the way she does now.

I felt my stomach coil as I read. This was the first time her obsession with Claire appeared, the first clear sign that she was planning. The writing was jagged, hurried, almost shaking with fury.

Nick doesn't notice how dangerous she is. I will show him. Clay will help. He knows what needs to happen. Nick has to stay mine. Claire needs to disappear. Soon.

I put the copies of the journal down, letting my fingers hover over the page.

My hands trembled slightly. I'd always suspected she hated Claire, but seeing it so starkly, written in her own words, was chilling.

Turning the pages, I came to entries about Jessica—a fan, nothing more than that.

06/20/2020 — That girl, Jessica... she keeps messaging him. He smiles at her, thinks it's innocent. Clay told me to watch. She's a threat. She thinks she can be close to Nick, but she can't. Not like me. I will handle it if I have to just like I did with Claire. I can't let anyone take what's mine. Not even a fan.

The words stabbed at me. I remembered Jessica's emails, her excited notes at signings. Nothing serious, but Lucy had turned it into a reason to escalate. Her handwriting was spiky, almost violent in places.

08/17/2023 — She's gone now. It had to happen. No one can ever be between us. Clay agreed, he's always on my side. Nick doesn't remember, but I do. I always remember.

I found entries about Clara:

11/13/2023 — She smiled at Nick. Barely anyone would notice, but I did. That's enough. He thinks it's just work, an interview for some podcast she runs. I can't allow it. Clay agrees, it's necessary. Nick would forgive me if he knew. No one should get close to him, especially not her.

Clay. That voice. The voice she always claimed protected me, always gave her the excuse to manipulate and act. I flipped the pages slower now, dread building—a more recent entry.

Nick's dad is back, and I know Adam had something to do with it. I've let Adam stay alive for too long, that was my mistake. Clay agrees with me, of course. He always does. Lately, I think I like Clay better than Nick... he listens.

"Jesus," I muttered, my voice low. "She was... she really saw everyone around me as a threat."

Adam glanced at me, tired but alert. "Yeah. She did. And she planned all of it. Every step, every interaction."

***

I looked down at the journals again. Each entry is a window into her twisted mind. Each line is a reminder that the girl I once thought of as a friend, maybe even a sister, had been planning, obsessing, and watching me my entire life.

"And Clay," I said quietly. "She used him for everything. Even now, part of me..." I trailed off, shivering.

Adam shook his head. "That's over, Nick. That part of her is gone. But the rest... we deal with it. One step at a time."

I didn't answer. The weight of Lucy's last words hung between us, heavy and final.

Thirty minutes passed, maybe more—before Adam finally spoke again.

"So..." he started carefully, "how are things with Clay?"

I gave a dry laugh, "You'd be surprised."

He looked up, waiting.

"You wouldn't believe me if I told you," I said, eyes drifting out the window. "On my way to Badwater Basin, I stopped in Utah. Angel Point. Met a hippie who offered me mushrooms."

Adam frowned.

"Nick, please tell me you didn't—"

"I did," I cut in. "I was already planning to disappear, so what did it matter? But after tripping...

I've never felt more in control. It's like everything made sense for the first time. And Clay?"

I smirked faintly, "I'm not too worried about him anymore."

Adam sat in silence, he looked stunned—like he'd heard the words, but they hadn't landed yet.

"I told you, you wouldn't believe me," I said, a half-hearted smirk tugging at the corner of my mouth.

"No, I believe it," he said finally, voice low.

"Just... trying to wrap my head around it all."

"I don't expect you to." My tone softened. "It wasn't just the trip—it was like I stepped outside myself. I watched everything I'd buried claw its way out. Clay wasn't a voice anymore. He's something I can finally look in the eye."

Adam frowned, his brow creasing like he was afraid to ask. "Face him how?"

"Like he's not the enemy anymore," I said, my gaze fixed on the peeling wallpaper. "Just a part of the wreckage I have to own."

He exhaled slowly and heavily, then gave a reluctant nod. "So, that's it then? Clay's gone?"

"Gone isn't the right word." I leaned back, eyes tracing the ceiling. "He's... quiet. Like he's waiting. But I'm the one steering now."

Adam's lips parted, then closed again.

"You found something," he said finally.

"Something that gave you perspective. Probably scared the hell out of you first, but... it cleared the static."

I nodded, the memory tugging at something deep. "Yeah. It wasn't peace exactly—more like acceptance."

Adam's voice lowered, "And Lucy?"

The name hit like a stone dropped into still water. My shoulders tensed before I could stop it. I looked down at the open journal between us, the ink on the page like fresh wounds.

"Lucy thought she could control what she didn't understand," I said quietly.

"Same as I did."

"Nick, I hope you're not getting sucked into the past right now. I mean, I get it, with everything that's happened, but if we're going to get away with this, we need to stick to the story. No changes. The police will have all the evidence when they investigate further into Lucy."

I nodded, letting the words sink in, trying to shake the memories that still clawed at the edges of my mind. And yet, it was impossible not to think about what came next—what life looked like after Lucy had faded from it.

The stillness of the motel room was broken by the sudden trill of the chorded phone sitting on the nightstand. Adam picked it up without hesitation.

"Hello?"

A voice came through, hesitant but firm.

"Where's Lucy?"

Adam's brow furrowed.

"Who is this?"

The voice lowered, colder,

"Lucy's brother."

Author's Note

This book explores themes of trauma, grief, and moments where Nick feels overwhelmed by the desire to disappear. While this story is fictional, the emotions behind it are very real for many people.

If you or someone you know is struggling with thoughts of suicide or self-harm, you are not alone— and help is available. Talking to someone can make a difference, even when it feels impossible.

In the United States, you can call or text **988** to reach the Suicide & Crisis Lifeline, available 24/7. If you are outside the U.S., please consider contacting your local crisis line or emergency services.

You matter more than you know, and there is support beyond these pages.

I hope the ending of this book didn't upset you. There are bigger plans for the next part of the story— more background on Lucy, and new challenges for Nick and Adam as they discover she has a brother.

I've already started working on it, but I won't give away any spoilers.

Some parts of this book were especially challenging to write. I don't have personal experience with dissociative disorders or extreme trauma, so I relied heavily on trusted websites, videos, and interviews to bring the characters and their experiences to life. I have faced my own past trauma. I do live with active anxiety and have faced periods of depression. So, I understand the weight of a racing mind, the panic that sets in, and the disassociation that comes from feeling overwhelmed.

The story shifts between Nick, his thoughts, Clay, Adam, interactions with Lucy, and Nick's dad. Each character shows different fears, motivations, and personalities, and I tried to make each one stand out while keeping them connected within the story.

I wanted to portray Nick authentically—not as someone with bad intentions, but as a victim of trauma and abuse. Some of the darker moments aren't easy to read, but they reflect realities we rarely talk about. I prefer to face the darkness rather than ignore it. Writing from his perspective was challenging; I had to step into his mind and explore his thoughts, emotions, and how he navigates the world around him.

Writing Nick's past trauma was one of the most emotionally difficult parts of this book for me. Although the events were fictional, I had to fully inhabit that pain in my mind to portray it honestly, which made some scenes especially heavy to write.

One of the hardest moments involved miscarriage. Miscarriages happen more often than people realize, sometimes suddenly and without explanation. Including this in the story was intentional—but deeply personal. I have experienced miscarriages in my own life, and writing those scenes meant revisiting emotions I usually keep private.

Nick's mother's response—her depression and reliance on alcohol as a coping mechanism—was written to reflect the depth of his trauma, not to suggest that everyone grieves the same way. Grief manifests differently for everyone, and this was one portrayal among many possible realities.

If you or someone you know is struggling with depression, I strongly encourage seeking help from a medical or mental health professional. I do not condone the use of alcohol or substances as a means of coping with grief or mental illness.

The shrooms scene required careful attention. I wanted it to feel authentic without sensationalism. While research supports psilocybin's potential to help with anxiety and depression, it is not a replacement for professional medical care, and anyone considering it should consult a qualified doctor.

The murder scenes were difficult to write as well. I'm not a killer, and I don't think like one, so inhabiting that mindset while keeping the story thrilling and believable took deliberate effort. The scene where Adam disposes of Lucy's body was particularly disturbing, but it felt necessary and worked within the story's context.

Researching law enforcement and crime procedures was fascinating for Adam's character. I wanted him to be a loyal friend to Nick while still grappling with moral dilemmas. Even when suspecting Nick, he pushed those thoughts aside because of their decades-long bond. I wanted that connection to feel real.

Lucy was probably the most challenging character to write. Everything she does is calculated, though eventually, she becomes impatient in her desire to have Nick to herself. I wanted her to be subtly obsessive—always present, never overtly obvious. Her death comes quickly, but it felt fitting. By the time she chooses to end her life, she has already shown Nick her true colors, leaving him no choice but to react. His rage when he "saw red" represents the release of all the emotions he had been holding in—the moment he finally breaks free from her influence.

Nick's dad also plays a difficult role in that conflict, but I wanted him to act out of love and protection—one final act for his son, showing the caring father, he always was.

Lilah represents the "speck of light" in this story. I wanted her to bring warmth, hope, and impact Nick's life meaningfully before her departure. Their relationship, and the bond that develops, is something I hope resonated with you—I even found myself moved to tears while rereading her sections.

Thank you for reading. I hope the story resonated with you in the best ways, and I can't wait to share what comes next.

Acknowledgements

This is my first book, and I wouldn't have been able to do it without the encouragement of my boyfriend, Chad. He nudged me to write, inspired me when I struggled, and supported me every step of the way. (Olive juice.)

I'm also deeply grateful to my children and my family, who have always supported everything I try in life. Special thanks to my brother Adrian, for showing that family means always having each other's backs.

To Mandy, thank you for reading the early chapters of this book and for the encouragement that meant more to me than you know. Your excitement, honesty, and belief in this story gave me renewed motivation when I was close to the finish line.

I want to thank Kayla for checking in on me throughout the writing of this book, even when I went MIA. Your support, encouragement, and gentle reminders kept me going on the toughest days—I couldn't have done it without you.

Finally, thank you to everyone who has read, given feedback, or cheered me on during this journey—your support means more than I can express.

About the Author

I write psychological thrillers and contemporary fiction that explore the human mind, trauma, and emotional complexity. Writing feels like home to me. It helps slow down my wild imagination and the thoughts that often run faster than I can keep up with.

I have many hobbies aside from writing. I love exploring all kinds of art, crafting, painting, photography, and traveling. These passions inspire me and feed my storytelling in ways that are always surprising.

Call to Action

If you enjoyed this book, I'd be thrilled if you left a review, followed me on social media, or shared it with a friend. Your support means the world and helps bring the next story to life!

Connect with the author at:
angelarose.writes@gmail.com